Under the Ginkgo Tree

——————————— • ———————————

An Anthology of
Traditional Japanese Short Form Poetry

by

Diana Barbour
Ann Brixey
Janet Foor
Ray Griffin
Debbie Johnson
Karyn Stockwell

ISBN: 9781792851933

Compiled and edited by
Ray Griffin and Ann Brixey.

Cover design and artwork © Marti Dodge.
3-Herons Art
www.3heronsart.com

Book design and layout by Ray Griffin.
This book is presented in Book Antiqua font.

Published in association with
Kindle Direct Publishing, Inc.
Printed in the United States of America.

Published by Ray Griffin in association
with and cooperation of the following poets:
Diana Barbour, Ann Brixey, Janet Foor,
Debbie Johnson, and Karyn Stockwell.

DEDICATION

To all
who enjoy reading
and writing traditional
Japanese short form poetry

And
particularly
to those who have
taught and mentored us
in these wonderful poetic forms

These
are the individuals
whom we refer to as
haijin, poet, teacher, friend

❧ • ❧

Alvin Thomas Ethington, *deceased*
Susan Galletti Campion

❧ • ❧

TABLE OF CONTENTS

TABLE OF ARTWORK AND PHOTOGRAPHY

ACKNOWLEDGEMENTS

It is with sincere appreciation and gratitude that the contributing poets and I acknowledge the following persons.

1) Marti Dodge, 3-Herons Art, for permission to use her beautiful art and particularly her stunning artwork for the book's cover and title page;
2) *Pixabay.com* for use of public domain designated photographs and imagery;
3) Elizabeth Shaw, for permission to use her beautiful photograph;
4) Robert Pridgen, for permission to use his beautiful photograph; *and*
5) Sherrie Hygon, for permission to use her beautiful photograph.

LIST OF PREVIOUSLY PUBLISHED POETRY & ART

The following haiku were first published in *Haiku Anthology: Observations and Insights* published by Douglas Paul Creations, LLC , 2017.

- white flakes swirl; woodpecker; ice fishers; and marbled nude; by Ray Griffin.
- ocean tide pool; tree frog's eggs hatch; newborn turtles; robins gather; and empty swing; by Karyn Stockwell.

The following poetry was first published in *Cattails Journal*, The online journal of The United Haiku and Tanka Society of America. *(http://www.cattailsjournal.com/welcome.html*:

- haiku: staycation; caesura; election day; *May 2015 Edition.* haibun: culture shock; wash down;

September 2015 Edition. tanka: moonlight filters; tanka: ocean waves; *January 2015 Edition*; eye of the storm; and daylight savings time; *January 2016 Edition*; by Diana Barbour.

The following poetry was first published in *Pieces of Her Mind: Women Find Their Voice in Centuries-Old Forms*, Omega Publications, 2012.

- snowman; nonstop voices; getting older; mirror mirror; mother's contain, and solitary star; by Karyn Stockwell.

The following poetry was first published in *Page and Spine*. *https://www.pagespineficshowcase.com/index.html*:

- storm warning, now titled: when shadows lengthen; flowers bloom; *16 December 2013 Edition*; time worn cobbled path; winter snowflakes; *18 April 2014 Issue*; morning serenade; Northwoods; *22 May 2015 Issue*; by Ann Brixey.

The following poetry was first published, in color, by *3-Hersons Art* as note cards in 2017 and is published by permission.

- haiga (beneath azure skies); artwork © Marti Dodge of *3-Herons Art*; haiku © by Ray Griffin.

The following poetry was first published in *Frogpond,* The Journal of the Haiku Society of America. *http://www.hsa-haiku.org/frogpond/*:

- haiku: ebb tide; *Spring/Summer 2015 Issue;* by Diana Barbour.

POETIC ART PRESENTED IN THIS BOOK

- book cover and art on title page © Marti Dodge.
- haibun art (the bait); photograph © Robert Pridgen; and excerpt from haibun (the bait) © Ray Griffin.
- haibun art (transforming); © Karyn Stockwell.
- haiga (as hillside snow melts); artwork © Diana Barbour; and haiku © Ann Brixey.
- haiga (beneath azure skies); artwork © Marti Dodge, *3-Herons Art*; and haiku © Ray Griffin.
- haiga (duality); © Ray Griffin.
- haiga (ginkgo leaves); public domain artwork, pixabay.com; and haiku © Karyn Stockwell.
- haiga (ripples); artwork © Diana Barbour; and haiku © Ann Brixey.
- haiga (luscious valleys); photo © Sherrie Hygon; and haiku © Janet Foor.
- haiga (late summer's soft light); photograph © Elizabeth Shaw, and haiku © Ray Griffin.
- haiga (naiads preside); © Ann Brixey.
- haiga (petals); © Ann Brixey.
- haiku suite art (awed); © Ray Griffin.
- kyoka art (the circus is here); public domain photograph, pixabay.com; and kyoka © Janet Foor.
- tanka art (wispy clouds); © Ann Brixey.
- tanka art (balancing act); © Janet Foor.
- tanka art (gunfire); © Diana Barbour.
- tanka suite art (mist shrouds); photograph © Ray Griffin; and tanka © Ann Brixey.
- tanka art (silvered lake reflects); © Ann Brixey.
- tanka art (in soft breeze); © Ann Brixey.
- tanka prose art (roots); © Janet Foor.
- senryu art (snowman); public domain photograph. pixabay.com; and senryu © Karyn Stockwell.
- senryu art (all day rain); © Diana Barbour.
- senryu suite art (mendacity); public domain photograph pixabay.com; and senryu suite © Ray Griffin.

'beneath azure sky
ginkgo sheds its golden leaves
synchronicity'

Ray G.

haiga (beneath azure sky)
– artwork by Marti Dodge
– haiku by Griffin

FOREWORD

Waka, the ancient Japanese word for poetry, has evolved into the beautiful Japanese short form poetry that we enjoy today. In the forms of renga, imperial court tanka, tanka, kyoka, haiku, senryu, haibun, tanka prose, and haiga are founded in the tanka's poetic roots dating at least to 12th century Japan. As the centuries progressed, so too did the art and form of writing these traditional poetic forms.

In the mid-20th and early 21st centuries, poets began experimenting with new genres known as modern or contemporary tanka and haiku. Part of the reason for this growing dichotomy in the traditional genre is the differences between the Japanese and English languages. Each allows for things the other does not. Also, the modern form tends to reflect a sense of Western poetry within its construct.

This is not to suggest that traditional is better than modern haiku and tanka, or vice versa. Each spoken language continuously evolves; consequently, so too does its written forms; its poetry. Thus, the poet has the opportunity to explore new genres of the form as well as to continue to write in the more traditional, or conservative vein.

As with any new genre of a poetic form, sometimes the experimentation in writing can evolve to a point unlike the original intent, or spirit of the form. Such was the case with the modernist movement during the 20th Century with blank verse. So too is the case in some instances with modern Japanese short form poetry.

The beauty of the Japanese short poetic form is in its tightly crafted observations, cut-lines, or satori, when appropriate, helps to lead the reader into another world. Well-chosen words and phrasing help ensure the reader will be able to see, to sense, and to contemplate the images and their deeper meanings being painted within the poetry.

Without a doubt, Japanese short form is not an easy poetic form for either poets or readers. The poet must be careful in phrasing thoughts in such a manner that it is not just a retelling of something being observed but does so in a way that allows the reader to go beyond the obvious. The reader must work at reading and understanding the poetry, pondering it and allowing the emotive impact and the insightfulness of it all to sink in.

In other words, in much of Western poetry, poets labor to explain everything away. Not much is left to the reader's imagination. The Japanese short form, however, allows the reader to become part of the poem and to inject himself/herself into the spirit, the essence of the poem.

Because of this dichotomy of Japanese short form poetry, traditional and modern, a small group of six poets formed into a Tuesday evening poetry group in 2017. Most of the group had been writing in traditional Japanese short form for years, and a couple of others were just beginning.

Our small group is known as the *Poets Corner*. We strive to focus on the more traditional approach to writing Japanese short form poetry. Our goal is to improve our craft through teaching and learning from each other.

In that vein, we seek to focus on concrete imagery versus the abstract. We seek to capture the essence of nature, of life through keen observation and effective satori. To help us achieve these goals, we concentrate on word economy and effectiveness versus elaboration in our haiku, senryu, kyoka, and tanka. We believe that excellence in Japanese short form writing focuses on the observations being made, and even more importantly, an effective satori. We enjoy writing of things beautiful, of love, of humorous things and events, of satire, life, and nature.

This anthology is based upon our study of the traditional tanka and haiku, and several forms associated with them. The book begins with tanka and continues with tanka related poetic forms of tanka suite, renga, imperial court tanka, and kyoka. The second half of the book focuses on haiku and continues with some of its related poetic forms, including, haiku suite, haibun, and senryu.

Dispersed throughout the book are haiga, haibun art, tanka art, tanka prose art, senryu art, and kyoka art. Also, each of the contributing poets provided a biography, and a short essay on what drives his/her poetry. One will find a short index at the end of the book.

I would be remiss to not recognize and thank the poets who contributed such beautiful poetry and art to this anthology—Diana Barbour, Ann Brixey, Janet Foor, Debbie Johnson, and Karyn Stockwell. Their talents have provided beautiful poetry through a diversity of writing styles and topics. And last but not least, I offer a particular *tip-of-the-hat* to Ann Brixey for her excellent leadership of our group, editing skills, and never ending support.

Thank you for reading our poetry.

Ray Griffin
January 2019

whispy clouds
glow in dawn's golden rays
interlaced
fingers as we walk
to our destiny

tanka art (whispy clouds)
– by Ann Brixey

TANKA

Originally known as waka, tanka is a poetry form which originated in Japan more than 13 centuries ago. The word tanka translates as "short song." It is equivalent to the sonnet in Western poetry. Thus, tanka is a beautiful, lyrical poetic form that often provides a strong emotive impact for those reading it.

Tanka is recognized for its simplicity, gracefulness, and succinct nature, more often than not reflects nature, and traditionally does not reflect violence or war images. It should include some deep meaning or purpose and leave the reader with strong feelings. Because tanka poems are meant to be given to someone, they are written from the viewpoint of the poet.

In its original form, tanka were written and enjoyed by the well-educated, and members of the imperial court. The form was used not only for pleasure writing, but also for official reports and communications between friends. Tanka became more widespread as it *spun-off* a new genre known as renga. Some of the other subgenres of tanka found within this book include tanka suite and tanka sequence. The humorous version of tanka is known as kyoka. Finally, a relatively new form, tanka prose, has gained significant popularity.

Tanka is a five-line poem with thirty-one syllables or less. It is usually one long sentence broken purposefully into five lines in a short–long-short-long–long format. The didactic tanka form taught in schools is to follow the 5-7-5-7-7 syllable count. While this is permissible in traditional tanka, the poet often uses less than 31 syllables and with varying syllable counts in each line, but still following the short-long-short-long-long format. Some additional guide-lines are provided below:

- Start with two lines that are haiku-like. They are grammatically connected and reflect a natural element. These two lines, along with line three, provide the external perspective of the poem. It sets the tone of the tanka.

- The third line changes the tone and direction of the tanka. This line must serve two critical functions. First, it serves as commentary, or satori, on the first two lines, and secondly, a pivot to begin the last two lines.

- Finish with lines four and five. These lines evoke an emotional reaction from the reader. The last two lines provide the internal perspective of the tanka.

- Tanka guidelines are more flexible than are the ones for haiku. The poet may use metaphor and/or simile, as well as personify nature. However, as with haiku, tanka admires word effectiveness and word economy. Capitalization and punctuation should be avoided except when absolutely necessary, i.e., proper nouns. Tanka does not utilize end rhymes or excessive alliteration.

—Janet Foor

Moscato grapes
hang heavy and ripe
cheers
to the vintner
for this sweet bubbly wine
— Foor

in a forest thicket
doe nuzzles her fawns
a wolf howls
shivers race
up my spine
— Foor

puppies play
in muddy puddles
happily
dressed in her white frock
Julie Marie cuddles each one
— Foor

purple clouds
fold over setting sun
bereavement
joyfully at reveille
I watch Sol rise again
— Foor

Biography

Janet Foor

Janet's life began in Northwest Pennsylvania not far from Lake Erie in a small town. Its billboard boasts, "The Biggest Little Town on the Map." She grew up with one sibling, a sister, in Youngsville, Pennsylvania.

Married after high school, she raised two children, Ben and Julie. When they were almost grown, she went to work at the county Emergency Management Agency which ultimately led to a job in Harrisburg with the Pennsylvania Emergency Management Agency (PEMA). She was the Operations Supervisor during the 911 attack on America. She deployed the Pennsylvania Urban Search and Rescue Team to the World Trade Center and coordinated an emergency response to Somerset County in Pennsylvania where the third plane in the attack crashed.

Janet is a wife, mother, step-mother, grandmother of 11 and great-grandmother of one. She is active in her church, loves yoga, gardening, cooking, entertaining, and her Irish heritage.

Janet did not discover writing poetry until after her retirement. Japanese Short Form poetry came even later when a friend introduced her to the form. This is her first inclusion in an anthology.

—JF

redbuds
emerge along the path
awakening
brilliant crimson blossoms
lift my spirits
—**Foor**

rising sun glistens
on placid mountain pond
birdsong
as beavers drag twigs
to build underwater home
—**Foor**

before dawn
on placid mountain lake
haunting
common loon wails
his eerie, ghostly call
—**Foor**

brilliant yellow ginkgo
sways in autumn breeze
sublime
are its leaves as they rain
down upon my just-raked yard
—**Foor**

apple orchard thrives
where farmhouse once stood
echoes
of children's laughter can be heard
in passing breeze
—Foor

lilac blossoms
droop from heavy spring rains
nostalgia
their sweet fragrance reminds me
of my lavender prom dress
—Foor

white curtained windows
adorn creosote-stained house
giggles heard
cousins nestle
in grandma's feather bed
—Foor

glowing sky
causes evening stars to wake
anticipation
of hope resides in twilight
as night caresses day
—Foor

moonlight glows
in twilight sky
exhausted
we sleep under the heavens
by the icy mountain stream
—**Foor**

lovers stroll
along sandy beach
enticing
my memories grow sweeter
as our unborn baby kicks
—**Foor**

verdant hues
creep over hills and valleys
transformed
I smile as sunrays and raindrops
tango in the distance
—**Foor**

morning haze
hugs eerie shoreline
Sol glimmers
through misty fog
revealing placid sea
—**Foor**

balancing act
with a different slant
rock on
wilderness graffiti
marks my path

tanka art (balancing act)
— by Janet Foor

daffodils
emerge from snow's deep shroud
everlasting
inspiration for man's heart
as is your soulful poetry
—**Griffin**

astral light glistens
on lake's rippling waters
reflections
of you wash over me
as I grasp your fading hand
—**Griffin**

late winter storm
enshrouds holly's red berry branches
bone chilling
was the news of your death
and loss of your friendship
—**Griffin**

lichen enshrouds
marble marker's inscription
memories fade
time and distance
mark their impact on my heart
—**Griffin**

rare night's orb
lingers over high mountains
blue moon
reflects in your azure eyes
as I pull you close
—Griffin

earth's rim aflame
as night sky envelopes
transitions
of life in so many ways
weigh heavily upon my heart
—Griffin

winter storm
colors landscape white
dry snow
makes no snowmen
I am alone tonight
—Griffin

wind-blown leaves
swirl in upward spiral
pirouettes
remind me of your steadfast
love as you pull me close
—Griffin

~tanka~

wind and rain
fall upon tin roof
symphony
awakens my soul
to new beginnings
—Griffin

we sip prosecco
amid banter and laughter
la dolce vita
embraces old friends
reconnecting after many years
—Griffin

frigid wind
bows weeping willow
grave's sentinel
welcomes me
as warm tears fall
—Griffin

thick ivy covers
campanile's ancient stones
enshrouded
my darkest fears
as I embrace dawn's light
—Griffin

11

Under the Ginkgo Tree

yesterday's rose
pressed between sonnets' pages
eternal love
he resides in your heart
and shall always be with you
—Griffin

sea shells revealed
by receding tide
a perfect conk
resounds life's echo
as I hold it to my ear
—Griffin

I hear Robin's song
as dawn crests Afton's ridge
soothing
to my frayed consciousness
as I dare think of yesterday
—Griffin

brilliant sunset
absorbs all that approaches
portal
through which we leave the old
in search of tomorrow's promise
—Griffin

sol ignites
as it descends earth's rim
illumination
I've never seen you
as happy as you now are
—Griffin

once mighty oak
decays throughout the centuries
a verdant sprig
sprouts forth reminding man
he's not judged by just one act
—Griffin

nature finds
a perfect balance
equilibrium
I am, I said
as I walk into tomorrow
—Griffin

leaves pirouette
onto still-verdant lawn
patterns
to ponder as I realize
life endures despite the odds
—Griffin

spring rains
nurture flora and fauna
rejuvenation
with love and respect
we can coexist as equals
—**Johnson**

in swift winds
raindrops cling to maple leaf
determined
I hold on to hope
through perilous times
—**Johnson**

blue
morning glories climb porch railing
nature's accessories
worn with
summer dress
—**Johnson**

rainbow's hues
replace dark storm clouds
endless spectrum
life's possibilities
on display
—**Johnson**

autumn leaves
scattered on grassy floor
gusty breeze
sweeps in a bitter chill
across my mosaic path
—Johnson

golden oak leaf
trembles in autumn winds
vestige
clings as advancing years
replace those of my youth
—Johnson

autumn's palette covered
as snowflakes fall
season's joy
while embers crackle
warming my poetic words
—Johnson

clear blue
water without a ripple
peace and serenity
can be found if we
search our inner being
—Johnson

a moonlit night
amongst the blossoms
summer's zenith
we enjoy a garden party
feasting on fruits of my labor
—Johnson

shifting clouds
enshroud October sun
mourning
I hold a faded photo
of my father close to my heart
—Johnson

dark clouds form
and rain pours from heavens
grief-stricken
tears stream down my face
upon losing my son
—Johnson

~ • ~

~tanka~

crimson leaves hang on
amidst rare October snow
premature
infant clings to life
with strength of mother's love
— **Stockwell**

dawn arrives with warmth
to banish chill of night
heat intensifies
as your fiery parting words
burn and scar my shattered heart
— **Stockwell**

solitary star
winks a nighttime greeting
welcome friend
I smile back at my twinkling
midnight companion
— **Stockwell**

spring bursts with color
after winter's isolation
waiting over
when new dad cradles his son
and feels his world reborn
— **Stockwell**

17

warm squishy sand
snuggles child's toes
impressions
of daughter's tiny feet
following in Dad's footprints
— **Stockwell**

midnight moon
creeps around the clouds
winking light
invites me to dance
to the music of night sounds
— **Stockwell**

rustic barn
stands deserted in Midwest
weathered
on once bustling farmland
abandoned by foreclosure
— **Stockwell**

snowflake ballet
in symmetrical beauty
enchantment swirls
with sweet dreams of dancing
the night away in your arms
— **Stockwell**

withered foliage
tumbles from oaks and maples
blanket of leaves
cover city park bench
where homeless man languishes
— Stockwell

filtered sunlight
dances through summer leaves
lacey patterns
of Gram's Irish lace curtains
making designs on parlor floor
— Stockwell

dawn's choir of chirps
announces spring's arrival
birdsong symphony
as I seek sanctuary
beneath my down comforter
— Stockwell

stunning beauty
in land of enchantment
Irish charm
welcomes my wandering soul
and inspires me to write
— Stockwell

Under the Ginkgo Tree

morning sun
sparkles on spring buds
blossoms ablaze
at every turn I rejoice
to witness nature's rebirth
— **Stockwell**

robin redbreast
chirps his song at dawn
crooner
serenades and I smile
to begin the day with music
— **Stockwell**

fierce winter storm
threatens the unprotected
footprints
of two deer trudging through snow
towards abandoned lean-to
— **Stockwell**

~ . ~

scent of petrichor
permeates the morning air
tears
fall as you pass away
in my loving arms
 — **Barbour**

moonlight filters
through the Venetian blind
ready for bed
I know the face in my dreams
will most certainly be yours
 — **Barbour**

ocean waves
crash along the dunes
on vacation
broken seashells remind me
of our uncoupling
 — **Barbour**

six hundred
pairs of eyes gaze upwards
mesmerized
only the word awesome
breaks the silence
 — **Barbour**

Biography

Diana Eileen Barbour

Born in Washington, D.C., Diana spent the first half of her life equally in Rockville and Frederick, Maryland. It was there that she developed her lifelong love of foreign language, the arts, music, and tinkering with and dabbling in this-and-that. Dabbler is the best word she's found to describe her approach to her varied interests. Never truly bored, one can always find her engaged in something. Oftentimes, she will pick up an old instrument or her drawing pencils after a long hiatus and begin her journey anew.

Through the years she has been many things and traveled to many faraway places. She has been a farmer's hand, a goldsmith, an entrepreneur, a petty officer, and a teacher. She has lived in Spain and France and has been fortunate enough to visit many other beautiful and unique places around the world as well as in this great country. These experiences have shaped her, and she had grown exponentially as a human being as a result.

A bit of a homebody these days, Diana can be found at home in West Virginia preparing lesson plans and grading papers, dabbling in whatever interests her, or simply relaxing on the couch with one of her six cats.

Several of her Japanese short form poems have been published in the online journals *Cattails,* and *Frogpond.*

—DB

wildflowers
adorn fields far and wide
midsummer
too soon recess ends
and class resumes
— **Barbour**

sunset
solemn notes echo
between gravestones
I consider who will
receive my colors
— **Barbour**

old jukebox
plays a sad song
I think of you
loosing myself
in our lang syne
— **Barbour**

anchored warship
rocks port to starboard
on watch
I pass the hours
walking bow to stern
— **Barbour**

north winds
whistle through empty fields
autumn
I kneel beside your grave
to tell you I am sorry
—**Barbour**

withered leaves
carom about the sacred grotto
God's altar
where I say a silent prayer
and light a candle
—**Barbour**

I lie on cut grass
daydreaming into late spring
azure skies
streaked with contrails remind me
of places I long to see
—**Barbour**

brumal fog
enshrouds mountain forest
on my own
I hear the sound of snowflakes
at the end of their descent
—**Barbour**

gunfire
errupts in the valley
covered ears
my little one asks
if Bambi's alright

tanka art (gunfire)
— by Diana Barbour

Under the Ginkgo Tree

deep in the greenwoods
tiny creatures forage
undisturbed
we gather wild mushrooms
epicurean's delight
— Brixey

when shadows lengthen
day slips gently into night
darkness envelops
old beech tree gnarled by time
owls hoot songs of the wildwood
— Brixey

dust motes
reflected in sun's rays
child's laughter
when dogs pace and paw at door
impatient for evening walk
— Brixey

dense clouds
roll down craggy mountainsides
storm imminent
when thunder reverberates
across fertile valley floor
— Brixey

storm clouds
scud across a leaden sky
vernal equinox
mother nature's last laugh
in so many areas
—**Brixey**

autumnal colors
viewed from hill top
crazy quilt
from grandma's bed
now proudly displayed
—**Brixey**

in strong winds
clouds race across ocean's surface
a vortex forms
storm's fury is unleashed
swimmers dash to safety
—**Brixey**

clear frosty morning
enhances autumn colors
breeze blows
pungent wispy smoke
into my eyes
—**Brixey**

Under the Ginkgo Tree

field mice
forage ripening wheat stalks
barn owl squeaks
I watch a wily fox pace
outside my darkened window
—Brixey

bluebells
bloom under woodland's canopy
hiraeth
fills my heart with desire
to wander there with you
—Brixey

shells litter
tide-washed secluded beach
footprints
lead me to your embrace
we celebrate our love
—Brixey

mist engulfs
ocean's tranquil surface
eerie silence
pierced by birds' incessant cries
solitude invaded
—Brixey

~tanka~

evening's cool breeze
stirs cherry blossoms
I shiver
in secluded tea house
the swish of silk kimono
—**Brixey**

hearty sandwiches
and icy lemonade
delicious
fare for summertime picnic
healthy appetites sated
—**Brixey**

wild winds
strip trees bare
natures force
scatters sodden leaves
upon the earthen mound
—**Brixey**

on cenotaph steps
a single poppy flutters
veteran steps up
his salute to fallen comrades
with head bowed I brush a tear
—**Brixey**

29

tanka suite art (mist shrouds)
— photo by Ray Griffin
— tanka by Ann Brixey

TANKA SUITE

The tanka suite follows the same guidelines as provided in the previous section for traditional tanka. With that said, tanka grouped together in a suite allow the poet to develop a more detailed story. Importantly, each tanka in a suite must be aligned and work well together. Additionally, each tanka must also be able to stand on its own.

—**Ray Griffin**

tanka suite (possibilities)

morning star
glimmers on mountain stream
light
as we prepare the bait
coffee brews

sun rises
over snowcapped peak
carpe diem
ready to catch rainbow trout
in fast-flowing stream

evening star
sparkles on dusky horizon
smiles
while trout sizzles
we sit around the campfire

—**Foor**

31

Under the Ginkgo Tree

tanka suite (winter)

shards of light
pierce the darkness
icicles melt
as buttery sun shines
through my window

rust colored leaves
lie frozen in puddles
icy chill
takes my breath away
in the frosty morning air

pine boughs bend
from heavy snowfall
cardinal sings
at the top of the tree
before he flies away

snow crunches
beneath my feet
hoary white
walkway leads me home
to hot chocolate by the fire
— **Foor**

tanka suite (autumn)

pink clouds
cover snow-capped mountain
eagles soar
on lofty currents of air
over the high country

October grasses
linger on the meadow
sunlight dwindles
as the sweet musky scent
of autumn fills the air

Canada geese
form V in the evening sky
undaunted
by the crisp arctic wind
they fly in formation

sol's soft mellow glow
streams from the northland
Indian summer
brings brief warmth
to the season's end
—**Foor**

Under the Ginkgo Tree

tanka suite (new waxing moon)

new waxing moon
lingers just above barren trees
impeccable
beauty such as yours
takes my breath away

razor-thin crescent
dips below mountain ridge
darkness
yields to brilliant stars
as we hold each other tight

constellations
bejewel the flawless night sky
alluring
as are your soft blue eyes
and tender kiss
— Griffin

tanka suite (summer rain pelts)

summer rain pelts
downtown's hot cobblestones
evanescence
the poem I dreamed
has disappeared from my thoughts

I write at night
beside Grandma's oil lamp
illumination
I see beyond the stars
as I write of things deep within my soul

fall leaves swirl
in autumn's northwest winds
teapot's tempest
my scattered words make no sense
as I scribe them upon the page

vineyard yields
most outstanding harvest in years
la dolce vita
I sip the vine
and pen a sonnet for my love
— Griffin

Under the Ginkgo Tree

tanka suite (leaves softly rustle)

leaves softly rustle
in autumn's lively breezes
robin sings
while we reap summer's bounty
and celebrate the harvest's home

conkers gathered
from horse chestnut tree's base
childhood memories
heightens my anticipation
of long winter's nights spent with you

horse chestnut's
hand like-leaves flutter to ground
waving goodbye
to the end of summer
and our childhood

winter's cruel winds
churn up driven snow-banks
for warmth
robin hides his head
and we snuggle together

tight buds
adorn leafless branches
season of rebirth
announced by robin's sweet song
from the hillside meadow
— **Brixey**

36

tanka suite (mist shrouds)

mist shrouds
bracken clad foothills
saturated
mossy scree covered trails
morning hike treacherous

the gurgling of a rill
and chirping of birds becomes
music
energizes me
on my early morning trek

sheltered
between craggy mountain peaks
tranquil lake
sparkles in noonday sun
dazzled ~ I shade my eyes
— Brixey

tanka suite (Sol's eclipse)

ocean waves echo
upon Pacific's rocky shore
entices
we await Luna's eclipse
of Sol's brilliant glow

heavens darken
as cool breezes kiss our faces
foreplay
excites our senses
as we entwine at noon's twilight

Sol and Luna
dance a perfect tango
melding
brings us closer
to our inner souls' love

sky lightens
as sun's diamond ring bursts forth
totality
of my heart and soul
as you say I love you
—Griffin

tanka suite (sun)

sun blazes
down on parched hillside
relentless
till thunder clouds bubble up
and lightning splits old oak tree

cooler mornings
herald fall's fast approach
refreshed
purple heather spikes
glisten in noonday sun

breezes sway
ripened seed heads
released
along with fallen fruits
orchard's bounty for wildlife

mist mutes
fall's vibrant colors
resilient
brittle leaves cling to branches
while ferns wither along pathway

fragrant smoke
curls upwards into pale sky
rekindles
memories of walks with you
through leaf strewn woodland paths
— Brixey

tanka art (silvered lake reflects)
— by Ann Brixey

RENGA

Renga is an ancient poetic form dating back at least to 12th century Japan. Contests would be sponsored by imperial, and governmental officials. These were important contests and poets who were invited to participate where indeed honored. It was also a form friends used to communicate with each other.

Jane Reichhold writes that tan renga simply means "short linked verse." *(Jane Reichhold, Narrow Road to Renga, 1989, pp. 1-10)* The shortest such verse is, of course, five lines, or one tanka. The first three haiku-like lines are written by one person and the last two lines are written by another as a response. The poetic form of the renga is a five-line poem with 5-7-5-7-7 onjis. An onji is the Japanese form of syllables, based on sounds. There is not a one-to-one correlation between the Japanese onji and the English syllable. The former is shorter and more precise. This is why one sees renga written in English with often less than 5-7-5-7-7 syllables, but always in a /short / long / short / long/long/ form.

Unlike Western poetry, the narrative in formal renga is not always linear. It contains many changes in direction, themes, points of view, etc. There is no beginning, no ending. Importantly, one poet writes the first three lines and the responding poet responds with his/her impressions and feelings. There is some order in renga through the placement of the moon reference, seasonal and flower references. However, when renga is used as correspondence between friends, etc., it does not follow these more strict rules. Thus writing, reading and understanding renga requires patience on the part of both poet and reader.

— Ray Griffin

renga (she glows with love)
– between husband and wife –
for Karyn

two flowers
thrive in morning sun
entwined
  I breathe you in deeply
  as we become one

spring's seed grows
as new life begins within
our renaissance
  is painted with joy and hope
  as new born babe breathes first breath

warm winter
yields early crocus blooms
fragile beauty
  is beheld as we see him
  lying beyond our reach

desert sand storm
enshrouds tomorrow's vista
eclipse
  of our hopes and dreams
  as prayers are lifted for him

soothing rain
clears sky as sun sets
God's strength
empowers his angels
to nourish and care for babe

moon wanes as
new life slips away
in my aching arms
I hold you both so very close
to my grieving heart and soul

thank God for caring
nurse who loved our son
God's embrace
touched us through our faith
and miracle of her love

she glows with love
while preparing him
angelic
nurse kisses our son's hand
as he ascends to Heaven
      — Griffin

renga (servant leader)
— between mentor and student —
for Bob

God's light
and a virtuous heart
   servant-leader
     manifests its essence
     only within statesmen

seeds of knowledge
planted and carefully nurtured
   enlightenment
     pulls us out of cave's darkness
     into wisdom's light

belief in man's
ability to thrive
   Jeffersonian
     liberal thought bestowed upon
     us through creative dialogue

in search of
methods to improve
   governance
     the body politic evolves
     by embracing others

belief in you
contracts your chiasm of doubt
   empowerment
     enables us
     to achieve exceptional things

a patient man
who counsels to one's varied needs
   venerable sage
      provides sturdy rudder amidst
      life's turbulent rapids

a stalwart man
who stands with you always
   friendship and commitment
      unconditionally offered
      to those who accept his hand

an honest man
who will not deceive you
   trustworthiness
      ethical governance
      demands nothing less

founders' vision
evolves for tomorrow's promise
   extraordinary
      liberty's institutions
      must be protected by us

time folds into itself
and leaves us on the edge
   evolution or devolution
      democracy's light fades when her
      people lose faith in themselves
              —Griffin

Biography

Ray Griffin

Ray is Southern by birth, Welsh, Irish, Scottish, and English by heritage, and a *repatriated* Virginian by choice. He was born and reared in Southeastern North Carolina but has also lived and worked in Virginia and Tennessee. It was while attending undergraduate college that he met his future wife; now married for more than 41 years. He is also the proud father of an adult daughter.

He served as a city manager for more than 38 years in five cities and retired on a Halloween Day. Ray enjoys genealogy and has researched and written four family histories. He is also a poet, and particularly enjoys writing in blank verse, sonnets and Japanese short poetic forms. He has taught meter, blank verse and sonnets to many students. Now, in retirement, he teaches American Politics at the local community college. Ray enjoys hiking in the nearby Blue Ridge Mountains, watching deer frolic in the woods behind his home, and enjoys spending time with family and friends.

Ray has had several haiku in the *Haiku Anthology: Observations and Insights* in 2017. Two of his poems, a Shakespearean blank verse sonnet and a free verse poem were published in the *2018 Bridgewater International Poetry Festival Anthology.* He has also published five chapbooks and is currently finalizing a sonnets manuscript for publication.

—RG

renga (deer tracks)

deer tracks
lead to shelter's lean-to
respite **(—Griffin)**
offers solace while storm rages
they snuggle in comfort **(—Stockwell)**

great horned owl
watches from giant oak
full moon rising **(—Foor)**
casts eerie shadows
on foraging field mice **(—Brixey)**

swaying branches dance
beneath night-time sun
lullabies **(—Johnson)**
I still cherish from when
you'd sing me to sleep **(—Griffin)**

fresh snow clings
to drooping boughs of blue spruce
cardinals huddle **(—Stockwell)**
lovers sit by the hearth
sharing dreams of Spring **(—Foor)**

smoke
curls up from hillsides
pilgrims gather **(—Brixey)**
turkey roasts over fire
tables set for Thanksgiving **(—Johnson)**

Under the Ginkgo Tree

renga (dewy tulips)

dewy tulips
sparkle in morning sunlight
rainbow garden (—Stockwell)
blooms on the hillside
makes my heart happy (—Foor)

confetti colors
replace winter's grey
meadow faeries dance (—Johnson)
beneath the star fields vivid glow
I ponder (—Griffin)

moonbeams
reflect on pellucid lake
swans glide (—Brixey)
resplendent beauty
arouses my errant muse (—Griffin)

morning mist
lingers over bucolic vineyard
tranquil sunrise (—Foor)
scent of fruit tantalizes
from sweet wine we share (—Johnson)

backyard songbirds
greet arrival of twilight
morning glories curl (—Stockwell)
night's choral symphony
begins as crickets chirp (—Griffin)

stars pierce
the indigo velvet sky
lovers kiss (– **Foor**)
before a tearful parting
and seas that come between them (– **Brixey**)

my toes in the sand
long warm days nourish
seeds of poetry (– **Johnson**)
emerge as remembered love
cast ashore like driftwood (--**Stockwell**)

fires blaze
atop promontory
signaling (– **Brixey**)
homecoming celebration
lovers reunite (– **Foor**)

morning sun
sets field of celosia ablaze
Picasso's palate (– **Griffin**)
brings a myriad of hues
for impressionist's paintings (– **Brixey**)

as flakes gently fall
bright landscape subdued
whitewash (– **Johnson**)
covering yesterday's roses
awaiting Spring (– **Foor**)

in soft breeze
ripples form on pond
petals scatter

a swish of silk
pretense falls aside

tanka art (in soft breeze)
— by Ann Brixey

IMPERIAL COURT TANKA

As early as the 10th Century, tanka was widely used among the educated, and members of the Imperial Court. One genre of the form, renga, provided for multiple persons to work together in writing tanka. The Imperial Court Tanka is a regna form of tanka and could be used as a way to communicate between lovers.

The morning after an evening of dalliance with a lover, well-mannered people of the Imperial Court wrote a thank you note for the hospitality of the previous night's assignation. It became customary to write in the convenient five lines of 5-7-5-7-7 *on*. The Japanese *on* is much shorter than the English syllable; consequently, it is not unusual to find tanka written in less than 31 syllables, but always presented in a short-long-short-long-long format.

The renga was most often, but not always, initiated by the woman who would pen the first three lines, and her lover would respond with the last two lines.

The verse would relate to the activities of the previous evening and would be couched in terms only the recipient would understand and appreciate. These poems would be subtly sensual in nature but would never refer openly to what had happened. This genre of Imperial Court Tanka is very creative in its use of metaphor and simile. Layered meanings, or double entendre, is also quite evident in this genre.

These little poems were sent either in a special paper container, written on a fan, or knotted to a branch or stem of a single blossom and delivered to the lover by messenger who, while waiting for a response, used the time to flirt with the household staff.

— **Ann Brixey**

51

Under the Ginkgo Tree

imperial court tanka (I sit)

I sit
in the pavilion
and wait
    lanterns glow and light the way
    along the cobbled path

full moon
glows above the tall bamboo
your beauty is enhanced
    in soft breeze sakuri swirl
    and fall into your lap

lotus flower rises
above broad leaves in dark water
and quivers
    butterfly koi
    nibble fragrant petals
            — Brixey

imperial court tanka (in soft breeze)

in soft breeze
ripples form on pond
petals scatter
 footsteps approach
 my anticipation heightens

branches
heavy with blossoms
 bow low
 while with a swish of silk
 pretense falls aside

halo
surrounds moon
 priceless
 as the rarest rubies
 your innocent blushes

at cicadas' cry
reality returns
 piercing
 darkened skies
 as an archer's arrow

in dawn's light
a flutter of wings
 the dragon retreats
 tears gentle as snowflakes
 fall on trailing sleeve
   — Brixey

53

Under the Ginkgo Tree

imperial court tanka (evenings cool breeze)

evening's cool breeze
stirs cherry blossoms
I shiver
in secluded tea house
the swish of silk kimono

lanterns
cast soft glow
on tranquil pond
against a dark sky
the crescent-moon rises

unencumbered
tea ceremony begins
the cup is proffered
on lithe limbs
sweet fruits ripen

soft flakes
caress your brow
as clouds obscure sky
the tap of your geta
fades like sighs
—Brixey

imperial court tanka (winter)

winter
snowflakes melt
on warm earth
while chrysalis
begins to stir

night is filled
with sound of shamisen's
sweet music
then butterfly emerges
from silken cocoon

the dragon
on my kimono
reaches for the crest
in moonlight's reflection
of dew laden buds
—Brixey

Under the Ginkgo Tree

imperial court tanka (your reflection)

your reflection
in pool's warm rippling waters
undulating
I bathe for you, my love
with scented flowers in my hair

I gaze upon your beauty
as my robe falls to the ground
yearning
I also feel your distant touch
and blush as I think of your kiss

oh lovely Luna
how you tease the lingering clouds
aroused
by your stance, I arise
from the pool and reach out to you

I swim towards you
with passion building in my loins
anticipation
of you holding me
close throughout the night
—Griffin

imperial court tanka (leaves ablaze)

leaves ablaze
beneath azure sky
perfect beauty
    of our love fills my heart
    as I walk along our path

golden leaves
cover once flowered meadow
forget-me-nots
    whisper in gentle winds
    where we loved beneath warm sun

mountain ridges
converge with brilliant sunset
portal
    through which we can reconnect
    despite our now different realms

eagle soars
towards earth's zenith
sacred
    moment when I feel your touch
    and kiss on cool night's breath

Venus shines
brightly in night sky
eternal
    love transcends this plane
    as I breathe in our memories
                  —Griffin

Under the Ginkgo Tree

imperial court tanka (wings spread)

wings spread
in elegant flight
butterfly
> *your graceful ballet*
> *entices and enthralls me*

in silence
I pause at your glance
captivated
> *by your soft blue eyes*
> *I yearn for your caress*

attracted
to love's tenderness
I linger
> *with you in my arms*
> *our bodies entwined*

I tremble
in your embrace
expectant
> *your fragrance excites me*
> *I breathe you in*

I blush in
anticipation of
your kiss
> *causes time to slow*
> *tides begin to swell*

— Stockwell & Griffin

imperial court tanka (my sweet night lady)

my sweet night lady
with scent of blooming jasmine
intoxicating
>   *this gentle elixir*
>   *that infuses each breath*

arousing beauty
outshines the moon's radiance
mesmerizing
>   *the deep gaze we share*
>   *as you draw me near*

your whispered words thrill
my heart like the nightingale's tune
transcending
>   *the great distance between us*
>   *until we embrace again*

last night's tender kiss
brought my desire to life
awakening
>   *the unquenchable flame*
>   *of everlasting love*
>   **—Stockwell & Barbour**

Under the Ginkgo Tree

imperial court tanka (flint is struck)

flint is struck
I cross the bridge
with faltering steps
    against the setting sun
    I watch as you approach

ripples on the pond
and cool breezes
calm anticipation
    impatient for your presence
    I reach your side

my heart flutters
as your hand takes mine
I sigh
    softly the moth draws closer
    to the flame

under velvet skies
glistening forms
dart amongst tall reeds
    as rising moon
    cast shadows on rippling water

the cup is offered
in the moon viewing pavilion
acceptance
    a silken rustle
    as crushed blossom falls
        —Brixey & Griffin

imperial court tanka (in twilight's haze)

in twilight's haze
thc bridge is crossed
anticipation
    of your tender touch
    in the soft lantern light

on the breeze
blossoms perfume night air
cicada chirp
    songs for you, my love
    in the evening mist

the cup
is proffered
fluttering leaves
    gently fall on the tea house
    where we first embraced

shadows lengthen
in the light of full moon
ice crystals sparkle
    your virile reflection
    an infinite gift to my loins
          —Brixey & Foor

Under the Ginkgo Tree

imperial court tanka (obscured)

obscured
by shadow of mountain
ice melts
in crystal stream
new life stirs

across
wooden bridge
plum blossoms
drop before they wither
delicate fruit revealed

as butterflies
emerge from cocoons
this tiny bird
flutters
in my
grasp

new dances
will be taught
performed
while shamisen
is plucked

as temple bells
reverberate
gardenia
in my hand
slowly fades
— **Brixey**

imperial court tanka (paper lanterns)

paper lanterns
cast dark shadows
bridge is crossed
    hem of your kimono flutters
    images of butterfly wings

sweet music fades
the night is still
fortune is revealed
    golden dragon
    reaches for eternal flame

ripples form
tendrils of willow branch
disturb pond's surface
    your grey eyes
    mirror water and stars

cup is empty
sake has been drunk
elegant garden no longer
    as lacquered fan snaps shut
    your serene smile fades
        — Brixey

I return to the house to top off my brew. I pause in the dawn's early light and am thankful.

dainty petals
dangle in the morning mist
suspended
in a time-warp
of treasured memories

tanka prose art (roots)
— by Janet Foor

TANKA PROSE

Tanka prose is a distinct poetic form combining two modes of writing, verse and prose. It is the *first cousin* to the haibun poetic form. While both poetic forms are similar, they are also uniquely distinct from each other.

While haibun is more of a journal method to convey a story, tanka prose is more poetic prose that utilizes more flowing sentences and some short phrasing. Because of this, tanka prose allows for the reader to effectively convey emotion, or in other words, compliment the tanka. Thus, it is an excellent poetic form through which to share memories, feelings, important events in one's life, etc.

There are three distinct yet interrelated parts to tanka prose—the title, the prose, and the ending tanka. The title should be unique and not be repeated within the prose or tanka. It should set the tone of the poetry as well as serve as a means to lure the reader into reading it.

The prose conveys the message the writer wants to share with the reader. It builds upon the title and develops the subject matter and represents an instant in time where something is happening. It may express an emotion which the reader can fill from his/her imagination. The prose is generally written in present tense, but it can also be written in past tense. Other than articles and conjunctions, words should not be repeated in the prose if at all possible.

The prose section can be of any length, but it is generally concise and not loquacious. At times it may be appropriate to present the prose in more than one paragraph. At all times the prose should be tightly focused, flowing and poetic with a sensory impression of taste, smell, sight, touch or sound.

Under the Ginkgo Tree

Tanka prose usually concludes with a tanka; however, sometimes a writer may choose to begin his/her tanka prose with a tanka, and some begin and end with tanka. The title should set the tone and direction of the prose, which in turn allows the tanka to build and provide closure to the poem. When ending the prose, the tanka must build upon the title and prose in a way that provides for closure of the poem. Other than articles and conjunctions, words in the tanka should not have been presented in the title and prose.

—Janet Foor

tanka prose (at day's end)

An on-shore breeze brings welcome relief from the oppressive heat. The setting sun casts long shadows. As weary families prepare to take their leave. Sand is brushed from sun bronzed legs. Belongings are gathered and the remainder of picnic food put into coolers. Damp towels are shaken, before being hastily thrust into plastic bags. Reluctant children, unwilling to give in to tiredness, wail. Their cries carry along the narrow strip of beach. Reluctantly they trudge behind their parents to hot waiting cars. A pair of lovers, arms entwined, stroll towards the worn dune path. A lingering kiss, and they too depart.

pelicans glide
over ocean's glassy surface
a sudden dive
and tiny fish disperse
tranquility prevails

Now the sea shore has been returned to its rightful owners. A flock of ibis fly in and jostle for the best spot. Wading in the shallows they search for tiny creatures. A Great Blue Heron strides purposefully along the water's edge. Finding a secluded area, he stops and patiently waits. High above, silhouetted against pink tinged clouds, a scarlet throated frigate bird rides the warm updraft. A sea turtle swims with the in-coming tide. When darkness falls, she will laboriously come ashore to deposit her eggs. She knows her spot.

tall dune grasses
sway in evening's cooling breeze
shoreline refuge
for nesting birds and wild-life
sheltered habitat
—**Brixey**

Biography

Ann Brixey

Born in Wales, Ann grew up in a musical family. From an early age she studied ballet. Her vivid imagination was nurtured and encouraged throughout her school years. In high school a lifelong love of literature and poetry was born. Guided by drama and dance teachers, Ann became a triple treat, singing, dancing, and acting in Amateur Dramatics.

After her marriage she moved to Canada with her husband and young daughter, and within several months she began teaching ballet. In order to qualify as an accredited teacher, Ann studied History of Dance, Pedagogy, Anatomy, Physiology and Psychology. Her imagination served her well for the writing of story lines for the ballets that she choreographed and produced. She continued teaching after moving to the United States and became Ballet Mistress for two regional Ballet Companies. When Ann accepted the position of U.S. Administrator for the Royal Academy of Dancing her teaching career ended. During her time with the Academy (RAD) she was directly responsible for writing newsletters for members and teachers in the US. This also included writing newsworthy items from the Americas for the RAD's international magazine.

After retiring to Florida, Ann began writing seriously. It was under the tutelage of haijn Alvin T. Ethington, that she developed a love of Japanese Short Form poetry. She has had works published in *Page and Spine*, and *Nature Writing Magazine*. Ann also enjoys writing short stories and is currently working on a novel.

—AB

68

tanka prose (silence)

In the eastern sky a full moon is veiled by soft pink clouds. The wetlands glow in the light of the fading sun.

Close to a bed of reeds, a Snowy Egret's yellow feet disturbs the water. This glorious bird ignores me as I approach, treading carefully and as silently as possible. My boots squelch in the boggy terrain. Chuckling to myself, I stop, wondering if I got stuck, who would see me. Hopefully not a passing gator! No, this part of the wetlands is brackish. These reptiles inhabit fresh water. I'm safe from that predator. All the while, I want to just sit and watch, but here in this quagmire there is no perch for a human. Ripened seed heads of the salt marsh grass sway in the twilight. One or two tiny birds cling to the stalks, feeding voraciously. A dragonfly alights on a bare twig and a cloud of tiny gnats dance above.

From the nearby beach a flock of Skimmers, disturbed probably by another human, take to the air. Along with passing gulls and terns their screeches break the silence. En-masse they block the golden orb that rests, seemingly precariously, in the spot where gulf meets sky. The noise disturbs the white form in front of me. A rush of wings and it disappears into the purple sky. Sol's golden glow captured on its wings.

as daylight
gives way to moon's glow
I wander
over verdant pathways
where once we roamed
— **Brixey**

Under the Ginkgo Tree

tanka prose (in my mind's eye)

The stately maples along Market Street created an arch over the walkway and gave me a welcoming sense of ease and comfort. Leaves of russet and burnt orange pirouette down in an elegant dance. On a gentle breeze, they spiraled to the ground. I watched my little girl, with her strawberry blond pigtails, frolicking in a kaleidoscope of colors. There were times when I couldn't distinguish the child from the scenery surrounding her. Seamlessly, she blended into the landscape in her pumpkin colored jumpsuit. Her bright green eyes flashed. Her toothless smile made me smile too. That impish grin could melt the coldest heart.

scarlet and gold
in autumn sun
my child's laughter
a memory to last my lifetime
and soothe a weary soul
—**Foor**

tanka prose (garments galore)

On this brisk morning, we head off to shop at the Outlet Mall. My 17-year-old grandson needs clothes for a photo shoot tomorrow.   One store, then two, another and more. We peruse each aisle of each one. Then back to the first to try on his best choices. A nice stripped sweater and khakis for a casual look. A different outfit for an evening on-the-town.   And finally, one for just hanging out with friends. Colors and prints. Blazers and knits. Jeans with holes and hooded jackets that match.   We laughed at the preppy displays that just don't suit him as we carry our numerous bags to the car.

Next stop, his favorite pancake house for dinner. What a fun day! And the best part – seeing him enjoy his meal before insisting on leaving the tip. I do believe this young man is growing up right before my eyes.

> joyfully watching
> boy's metamorphosis
> haberdashery style
> we bought copious attire
> and not a stitch for me
> **—Foor**

Under the Ginkgo Tree

tanka prose (reflections)

I awake early, get up, and peer east beyond my window blinds. The sky is layered with streaks of cobalt blue and stars caught between the stacks of color-shifting clouds. Sol's slow rise infuses twilight with streaks of light that changes from neutral grays and blue-black to magenta within the blink of an eye. The transition continues with the most vibrant blood-orange skies stretching towards the zenith before the sun's white-yellow glaze pierces sky's ever-changing face. I am amazed how dawn's kaleidoscope morphs by the second as I gaze upon heaven's gate.

I feel so very small as I gaze upon the firmament brewing in dawn's glow. Such radiance affirms the power of His hand over all. I am awed and bow my head. My muse beckons me to take my pen and scribe upon the sketchbook's leaves my deepest inner thoughts. I write of how I'm captivated, gazing upon Aurora's dance. As time races forward, my mind leaps back to when we walked upon the ridge so many years ago when life was full and morning's sky aglow; filled with a radiance I've yet to see again.

willow thrives
despite summer's drought
resilience
love survives the darkest night
and life's deepest chasm
—**Griffin**

tanka prose (portal)

The day has been quite unsettled with shifting clouds and continual gentle rains. I too am restless as I sit on pier's edge. The Sangiovese soothes my senses as descending mist begins to encroach upon lake's placid domain. All is quiet except for the occasional call of a loon. I skip-a-stone across water's surface just to create movement and sound upon this liquid sheet of glass. I relish the moment. My eyes follow the ripples until they disappear into the misty void. The fog thickens as the sole cry of a hawk, unseen, pierces the silence, echoing off of the nearby mountains.

I take my bottle, drinking from its neck, and settle into my red canoe. Slowly, I paddle towards the morphing void. As I pass through its edge the pier disappears. I place the paddle at my feet. The eerie quietness of the moment is disturbed only by the gentle lapping of the lake upon my craft. I am adrift in my thoughts.

sol briefly
pierces cloud's grey-white mantle
pathway
though opacity
provides poetic transparency
—**Griffin**

73

Under the Ginkgo Tree

tanka prose (somewhere in time)

I sit in firelight's glow. Classic FM plays quietly on the radio. A cup of tea warms and sooths. Outside, low clouds scud across a leaden sky. The brutal wind ruthlessly strips leaves from the Crepe Myrtle. It sways the sapling Chinaberries like barren twigs. My notebook rests on my lap, my pen left on the side table. Languid. My eyelids heavy, I close my eyes — transported to another place.

The air is balmy, softly perfumed. Gentle breezes rustle through the weeping willow. Wavelets lap gently on the narrow grassy beach. A Nightingale sings its sweet trill. Robin Redbreast lands on a chair back. With bright eyes, he gazes at me. After a final aria, he departs to his home. In the twilight, bubbles in my wine glass seem to dance. I sip, savoring its clear dry taste. Then sigh.

sweet music
wafts across the lake
moonlight
reflections on silvern water
becomes a visual sonata
— Brixey

tanka prose (reflections)

Thunderheads are building up in the Southwest. But so far it remains calm. The sweet smell of Jasmine and Bee Balm mingle, perfuming the air. Lulled by the evening's tranquility, my notebook remains closed on my lap. I watch and laugh at the squirrels' antics. Undaunted by failed attempts to get past the baffles, they continue to climb the pole to reach the rich store above. Eventually thwarted, they forage on the ground. Every now and then I see one scamper through the grass to recover a distant tasty morsel.

A hummingbird lands at the nectar feeder. He feeds copiously. Sated, he quickly departs. A Blue Jay and several other birds swoop down to the seed cages. For a few moments, a minor skirmish breaks out. The victors, a brilliant Cardinal and his dowdier mate, are left to enjoy an early evening treat in peace. A clap of thunder. The squirrels clamber onto the pool screening and scurry away. Another rumble. Now I am quite alone. The breeze picks up. Dark clouds cover the setting sun. I lift my glass in a silent toast.

bees thrum
among the flowering shrubs
enticing
perfume reminds me
how much I miss your smile
—**Brixey**

tanka prose (paradox)

The sandbar jets out into the inlet. A large piece of driftwood rests in the sand making a perfect place to sit and watch the sun set into the sea. In the distance, an active volcano is spewing black puffs of smoke into the otherwise pristine air. Seagulls circle overhead, swoop down to catch their dinner. A flock of snow geese skim the icy water as ribbons of pink and gold drift over the horizon. Behind me, a windswept hillside reveals the effects of the severe northland weather. Perched on my speck of land with no human in sight, I am mesmerized by the enormity of the world and how finite I am.

the tide ebbs
revealing a *clam show*
surprised
I find this harsh seascape
is nourishing and calm
—Foor

tanka prose (roots)

Coffee cup in hand, I enter the garden and pick my first bouquet of lovely Lily-of-the-Valley. The white bell-shaped flowers hang from their tiny stems. Their sweet fragrance transports me back to momma's house where they freely grew under her dogwood trees. Each spring, I chose a spray of the delicate blossoms to carry in my stubby fingers and proudly put in her favorite vase.

A robin fledging startles me as he lands on the birdbath. He sits, perched and ready for his plunge. Splashing and flapping his wings, he retreats to the water's edge. I smile. I guess he wasn't prepared for a cold shower.

As the sun rises and turns the sky to a golden glow, I return to the house to top off my brew. I pause in the dawn's early light and am thankful.

dainty petals
dangle in the morning mist
suspended
in a time-warp
of treasured memories
—Foor

Under the Ginkgo Tree

tanka prose (whispers)

The predicted deluge arrived shortly after lunch in the form of a somewhat determined, but not torrential downpour. Muted thunder echoed off nearby mountain ridges in a stoic rhythm as raindrops slowly sifted through the trees with most delightful sounds. It was as though Beethoven was conducting his symphony and a choir singing lyrics composed by the master himself. I found myself drifting off into a muse-enhanced trance as I listened to storm's music play while cocooning myself in a padded old wicker chair on the back porch. Another sip of bourbon to bribe the quill. The rain becomes more gentle in what we Southerners call a soaker. It gently pings upon the window panes. I look beyond my perch and see three deer nestled in the leaves at the bottom of the yard beneath the oak. I hear a poem amidst a heavenly choral descant...

amid the clashes
of foreboding clouds
reprieve
for nature's life; my muse
as I begin to write
—**Griffin**

tanka prose (respite)

Oh, thank goodness, my muse is with me again after weeks of absence. I know not where she has been or with whom she has played. I feel her presence as I sip Grey Goose beneath my wonderful old oak late this afternoon. Though humidity is high, the shade and coolness provided by the tree are refreshing. Invigorating. Inspiring. Arousing. Juices flowing. My stylus is filled with ink. I pour myself another tonic and listen to the sounds of nature as my muse gently kisses my lips. Crows caw. Squirrels chatter and dance aloft on the myriad limbed oak. Jumping here—scurrying there! The white-noise of chirping birds, buzzing bees and other earthly things creates a jazz-like dissonance as the trees and shrubs gently sift soft northern breezes across my courtyard. I am immersed in the now but yearn for that which eludes me. My pen flows incessantly…

setting sun
gently casts soft, long shadows
portals
through which I must pass
to find my destiny
—Griffin

Under the Ginkgo Tree

tanka prose (we'll keep a welcome)

This warm, early spring morning found us driving through the foothills of the Eryri National Park. Eager to explore these splendid surroundings, we parked. An old footbridge led us to a stony trail. We ambled along. In hushed tones, our conversation was of old tales of dragons and beasties. When we found a comfortable spot, we sat.

The sun, a spinning orb, in the azure sky beat down. White clouds lazily capped the tops of the surrounding mountains. A carpet of wildflowers cloaked the riverbank. Water splashing down on ledges sang in merry counter-point to the sweet song of the birds. The river, swollen by the early spring thaw, and recent heavy rains, tumbled over its rocky bed. Decaying leaves and twigs bumped and swirled as they swept downstream to the waiting sea. Tranquility. My mind wandered. Suddenly it was quite cool and damp. The morning's warmth had gone. A mist had rolled in. I shivered but was reluctant to leave this comfortable spot. Traffic sounds had become muffled. The world became strangely still and silent. If Merlin himself had appeared I would not have been surprised.

at eisteddfod
bardic Welshmen gather
untold legends
keep past glories alive
and songs ~ music in our souls
— **Brixey**

tanka prose (Florida's summer's day)

A sudden drop in temperature from the mid-nineties to the mid-seventies made me shiver. The wind buffets the branches of the Chinaberry tree, and whips leaves and remaining blossoms from the Crepe Myrtle. Ominous dark clouds race across the sky.

Feeling chilled, I scurry to fill the kettle with freshly drawn water, put it on to boil then prepare a tray. Fragrant tea leaves are measured into my cherished Blue Dawn tea pot. A pale blue polka dotted cozy, lovingly embroidered with Bell flowers and butterflies stands next to it. These are reminders of childhood afternoon teas in the big farmhouse kitchen. Instead of a delicate bone china cup and saucer, today I opt for a mug with a winter scene of a robin in the snow.

With the storm at its height and cup of tea in hand, I relax in my easy chair reveling in its comfort. While the rain lashes at the windows, I sip the amber liquid and reminisce.

rainbow's
iridescent arc
brightened skies
entice us outside
for an evening stroll
— **Brixey**

Under the Ginkgo Tree

tanka prose (my Lucy moment)

This was the morning for cleaning the master bathroom. I turn on the faucet and depress the stopper then remembered the new cleaning products were in the kitchen. Off to retrieve the bottles. Heading back to the bathroom, I hear my husband arrive home from the store. Stopping in my tracks I help him unload bags of groceries. 'Beep.' my laptop announces a new message. I check and answer it, then move on to check my email. Before I know it, a half hour has passed. Time to get back to the work in hand. As I return, I see water running over the counter. It feels like a sauna. A deluge of rivulets inundates everywhere. With my feet already soaked, I pull the plug and grab all the towels. After mopping as much as possible, I wring them out in the shower and then slap them back on the still saturated floor. I throw them into a basket and head to the laundry room.

"No dear," I said, as I pass my husband in the hall. "No problem, I'm just doing a load of wash". I'm also hoping he didn't notice the dripping. Returning to the disaster area, I walk by the basement door. Hummmmm. Slowly I open the door. Panic strikes me as I see a lake below surging across the room. Gathering more towels and a mop, I race down the stairs wishing I had an Ethel to call for help.

a spring erupts
cascading down the hill
circuitously
I seek my own level
immersed in life's deep current
— Foor

tanka prose (polar express)

As I walk across the frozen meadow bundled in my red woolen coat, the sun slowly rises above the pre-dawn haze. I feel the snow crunching under my feet. A young doe quietly grazes on last year's grasses. Looking up with a start, she leaps across the pasture, her white tail flying in the chilly air. Jumping the fence, she disappears into the forest. Paw prints surround an old oak tree where squirrels had been collecting acorns in preparation for the long winter to come. Magpies chirp in the distance searching for berries. Over the nearby lake, the day takes on an amber glow as daybreak transforms the landscape into a mystic scene. One after another, mallards land on the frosty water, diving and searching for breakfast.

Giant snowflakes cover my path. I pull my jacket up around my neck and secure my earmuffs and gloves against the frigid wind gusts. I was happy that I had worn my turtleneck sweater and my long johns for my stroll in this, chilled to the bone, weather. I turn and head home for some steaming hot chocolate and the warmth of my crackling fireplace.

flurries of white
fell on the countryside
visions
of Santa and sleigh bells
crept into my head
—Foor

Under the Ginkgo Tree

tanka prose (simple pleasures)

It's late October and Indian Summer has finally ended. Today is cold, grey and wet. The drizzle is steady. The adjoining forest's foliage is ablaze in a kaleidoscope of brilliant reds, deep magentas, verdant evergreens, stoic browns, and luscious yellows and golds. I decide to walk out onto the patio to breathe in the fresh, cool air and feel the falling moisture upon my face.

As I open the door, I notice six deer foraging acorns beneath my venerable oak tree. Their color has changed from the warm, honey brown of spring and summer to an ashen grey. I am mesmerized as they put on a rare show of acrobatic beauty, frolicking along the edge of the woods, running and chasing each other. Leaping and bounding. White tails standing tall. I am transfixed.

An elder doe senses my presence. She cautiously approaches. Stopping...she looks me square-in-the-eye. Ears cocked forward. We stand still and watch each other as the herd returns to grazing upon autumn's fruits. I breathe deeply, quietly, as I see my muse within her eyes.

gentle rain
sets myriad leaves adrift
inspiration
overcomes me as I observe
nature in perfect harmony
        —**Griffin**

tanka prose (faith)

It's late. I cannot sleep. Snow and sleet dance on my window panes. The randomness of the pinging has no rhythm, but its syncopation creates its own melody. Soothing. Icy jazz...perfect for sipping another glass of red wine and contemplating what's next as I try to pen a poem. I am lost in my own thoughts as I ponder next week when I meet the surgeon's steel. A rush of whining wind whips 'round the edge of the house. Pensive. Lovely. My heart skips a beat...again.

I look out the window and see the porch light illuminating ice-glazed cedars along my courtyard's circuitous path. They glisten as though they were hand-dipped in Waterford crystal. How vibrant is their beauty juxtaposed against this brutal weather!

hash winter storm
pelts Afton with ice and snow
unsparing
dysfunctions of old age
succumb to life's hope and God's grace
—Griffin

85

Under the Ginkgo Tree

tanka prose (footprints)

Early morning. The beach seems deserted as the sun rises higher in the sky. In the distance, I see the person I call *the shell gatherer*. As she gets nearer, I notice something different. Today, no grocery bag hangs from her arm; nor is she stooping to pick up shells. Her shoulders are slouched, head down. There is an air of dejection about her. She stops and looks out on the tranquil sea. A furtive step into the lace fringed water. I hold my breath as she takes another. What is she thinking? Not the unthinkable? Please let it be my overactive imagination.

My own heart is pounding, and my mind whirls. The tide is coming in. She is nearing the drop off point. Although the waves seem playful, one or two reach her knees. From my balcony ten stories up, there is no way could I reach her quickly. No one to signal to. One solitary cloud covers the sun. The ocean no longer sparkles. I can only pray, "Dear Lord Help!!" She takes a step further. Suddenly on silent wings a Great Blue Heron lands beside her. She turns to look at the bird as a golden ray lights them both. A shake of her head and a look back toward the horizon. Then with the hem of her long skirt clinging to her ankles she walks along the sand. I say a silent prayer of thanks.

life's problems
seem insurmountable
contemplation
to dispel lingering doubts
and present inner peace
— Brixey

86

tanka prose (murmuration)

The sun is sinking closer to the horizon. The foot path seems never ending. Not wanting to miss the daily display, we hurry along. Breathless. Finally, our destination is in sight. Several other spotters are already there, field glasses in hand. Some already scanning the sky. Nods are exchanged. No-one wants to break the spell. We stand in the cold, muddy field. The only sound, squelching foot-treads as others join us. With camera adjusted I wait. Expectantly.

Twitterings and a sudden rush of wings breaks the silence. Uncountable, thousands of birds pass overhead. More land on a pylon behind us. Then, a hush. We wait with bated breath. No-one makes a sound. Suddenly, like billowing smoke they drift into the air. Veering right, left they continue. Rising high. swooping low. They disappear from view. We turn around and look up. As though by some pre-ordained signal, the remaining perched birds start to flutter. They bank westward. We view another display as incredible as the previous one. The sky and setting sun are obliterated by the swirling black cloud. Seconds turn to minutes until before our eyes, this mass also disappears into the tall grasses.

swaying fronds provide
safe haven for flocking birds
night-time display
amazes onlookers
I watch, humbled

— **Brixey**

tanka prose (stranded)

It's late summer on the Kenai Peninsula and the salmon are running. My alarm rings at 3 am. After a quick cup of coffee, I leave the cabin to claim my favorite fishing spot. The air is brisk. I begin to wish I had stayed under the covers dreaming of the fish that got away. The mouth of the Anchor River crosses over grass-covered mud flats and empties into the Cook Inlet. Since the sun never completely sets this time of year, I walk in its subdued light, following the path to the river. Across the inlet, snow-covered Mt. Iliamna glows a mellow candy-cotton pink.

I was not the first to arrive on the river. In fact, there was a crowd of fishermen, women and children already there. I decided to walk on toward the inlet and find an isolated spot. I crossed a field of fireweed with wild lupine growing on both sides of the path. The sky continued to brighten as I waited for the time when I could legally cast my line into the shallow Anchor River.

By 9 am, I had caught my limit of Dolly Varden Trout and three Silver Salmon. Time to start back to the cabin. In the excitement of the morning, I didn't notice the river rising. Soon, I was surrounded by water, standing on a little ridge that hosted some straggly shrubs. With my heart pounding, I wondered, "what do I do now"? Checking the Tide Chart in my pocket, I learned that high tide was 10 am. If I just waited, it would start to recede and free me from this lonely spot.

shoreline estuary
disappears into the bay
marooned
on a sandbar, I wait
for the ocean to ebb
—**Foor**

88

tanka prose (deck the halls)

I marvel at every adornment as each has a story to tell. The lovely gold heart with shiny stones that I bought in Paris and the blue felt "Bobby" from England for my husband Bob. There's a sweet clogging lass reminding me of my Irish heritage but all of them special to me. I lovingly suspend the crocheted snowflakes that my mother made, and the snowmen and candy canes fashioned by my children when they were young. I laugh as I see the Disney characters beside the brand new "pineapple" ornament sent from a friend in South Carolina. Tears of joy fall as I reminisce over Rudolf that always hung on my childhood tree. Then tears of sadness as I find a place for the iridescent baubles that were a gift long ago from my now estranged son. So many memories fill me as I trim the giant blue spruce. Christmas is coming – excitement fills the air.

a star
shines in the East
a baby is born
I ponder God's grace
in awe and wonder
—**Foor**

Under the Ginkgo Tree

tanka prose (stiff chocolate icing – part 1)

I am transported back in time as I walk within the remains of mom's old home. Oh, how it was once grand when people I loved lived here when I was but a boy. Its roof, peeled-off by Bertha's wrath in '96, has exposed its core to the elements. Decayed floors are dangerous as I walk through its rooms. They are now filled with trash — waste from owners who have cared not for the love and tradition it sustained since 1890. The odor of rotting wood and water-logged textiles takes my breath. I weep as I walk down the long hall, dodging gaping holes while remembering Aunt Mary greeting me with a hug at the front door. I look out at the old garage and see Lila's light blue bug parked by its gate. Oh, how good it is that Judy's snake jars are long gone! I remember playing under the house, and Uncle Hewett shaving outside and telling me about the Blue Jay in the front tree. I reminiscence of when we took Katie and Jack there for a picnic on the front porch back in 1970 — their last visit to her childhood home.

I sense a oneness with this place that I cannot explain. Lewis is removing still useful 120-year old clapboards for reuse in a new home — at least part of the old house will be repurposed in a good way.

withering tree
succumbs to life's storms
transitions
for home place and memories
as I walk around its impending grave

— **Griffin**

tanka prose (stiff chocolate icing – part 2)

But yet, I walk through the place a second time to reaffirm, reanimate my memories of that which once was so very sweet—so wonderful. My mother playing the old upright piano near the parlor's fireplace. My great-great-grandparents' house next door. Abandoned. Though I am now an old man, grey of hair and slow of stride, I can still smell the sweet fragrance of the baking cake wafting throughout the house. The kitchen's walls, now a faded pale green on battered, beaded board still beckon to me. I close my eyes and can see where she stood blending batter and spices into a mix that would rise into the best cake I have ever tasted. A home so comforting to me when I was very young. I cry aloud. Such shall never be again.

I exit by the back porch steps and ponder can how it is that she and her cakes bond me so to this place, fond memories, and where my kin were born and reared?

grape vine's expanse
is but a skeleton upon its truss
remnants
of when life was in full hue
and I played by lane's tall cedar
—Griffin

Biography
Debbie Johnson

Debbie does not remember a time when she could not read and used books as an escape from a troublesome home life. Her second-grade teacher was impressed with her writing and said she would write a book someday. In sixth grade, an essay she wrote on using natural dyes was published in the Palimpsest, an Iowa history journal.

After graduating with a degree in Food and Nutrition-Dietetics from Iowa State University, work and family left no time for writing, and not much for reading.

In 2004, at forty-one, she was disabled in an accident. In 2008 she had the opportunity to take an online writing class, *Writing through Change*, to help those with disabilities express themselves. The next year she joined a therapeutic writing group. She currently facilitates the group and leads a poetry group at her church.

Her two books, *The Disability Experience* and *The Disability Experience II*, are collections of poetry and prose. *Debbie's Friends* is a book she has written for elementary students about the need to treat the disabled. She's edited a poetry anthology written by the disabled.

She has had both poetry and prose published in Literary Journals and anthologies. Her Japanese *short forms have appeared in Ribbons, Bright Stars, two Tanka Society of America anthologies. Prune* Juice, *Atlas Poetica, Undertow Tanka, Neon Graffiti,* and *Page and Spine.*

Debbie currently lives in Nevada, Iowa with a very spoiled beagle. Besides writing, she gardens, enjoys crafts, and does disability advocacy.

−DJ

tanka prose (hireath)

It's dark-thirty. I am wide awake. Restless leg syndrome has kicked in, and my mind is fully awake. So much to think about, contemplate before I begin my trip home later this morning. A gentle drizzle begins to fall. I follow the gentle falling rain to where it leads me...

night becomes day
as rain sifts through trees
soothing
memories of a time
that no longer exists

It has been many years since I last visited this once beautiful, vibrant place built upon a minor promontory above the river at its confluence with the bay. Four-hours in the car seemed to fly by. Memories. Stopping at the entrance gate to the old plantation, I step out of my car, close my eyes and breathe deeply. Why is it that the scent of home never truly leaves a person? As I touch one of the four stone chimneys where my ancestral home once stood, I sense the fragrance of her perfume wafting in the gentle breeze...

fields have yielded
to encroaching forest
forty years
yet I still feel one
with you, and this place — home
— Griffin

the circus is here
with lions, tigers and bears
rumor has it
that it's not over
until the bearded lady sings

kyoka art (the circus is here)
— photo by pixabay.com
— kyoka by Janet Foor

KYOKA

The Japanese short form of kyoka, a subgenre of tanka, has been found to be written as early as the 8th century, but it peaked in popularity during the 1700s. Kyoka, translated as crazy, wild, mad, or playful verses, was frequently read at banquets and aimed at selected guests, similar to present day celebrity roasts.

Kyoka is often referred to as a sibling to the tanka format. The *rules* for kyoka are more flexible, but the form follows some of the requirements of tanka. Kyoka is usually written using five lines with thirty-one or less syllables employing a line syllable arrangement of short-long-short-long-long syllables. The form doesn't require a pivot third line as in tanka, but it is frequently integral to the poem. As with many other Japanese short forms, capitalization is used for only proper nouns, and punctuation is used sparingly.

What gives kyoka its distinct characteristics? The fun! The form allows the writer to whoop it up with creative freedom by using slang, puns, wordplay, parody, irony, and even silliness. Kyoka can be written to express satire with exaggerated humor or dark sarcasm and ridicule. Kyoka is to tanka what senryu is to haiku.

With no limits on topics, kyoka poetry offers both the writer and reader opportunities to discover the diversity and enjoyment of this Japanese short form. It may be termed the off-key stepsister to tanka, but the tones kyoka produces are certainly entertaining and provides an escape from the usual.

—Karyn Stockwell

nonstop voices
gossip in my head
mad tea party
of incessant chatterboxes
who lie through my teeth
— Stockwell

getting older
has its unique beauty
soft and comfy
like a worn saggy couch
a perfect fit for a weary butt
— Stockwell

mirror mirror
clever master of disguise
beauty magician
who conceals lines and wrinkles
by just closing your eyes
— Stockwell

solitary star
winks a midnight greeting
welcome love
I reach out to embrace
my memory foam pillow
— Stockwell

Mom, how come swimming
makes my willy so tiny?
with wisdom she says–
go ask your daddy, honey
he knows all 'bout the small stuff
— Stockwell

dry cleaners
has big after Christmas sale
dirty Santa suits
given half price discounts
fireplace soot and ash extra
— Stockwell

911 please help
I think my wife is dead
sex is the same
but dirty laundry and dishes
are piling up around here
— Stockwell

slinky stilettos
purchased in every color
sexy obsession
I don't dare use them to walk
recreational footwear
— Stockwell

97

Biography

Karyn Stockwell

Born and raised in Buffalo, New York, Karyn moved to Northwest Indiana as a young teenager and has remained in the land of corn and cows ever since. While trying to find her identity as a flower child, she changed Karen to Karyn to remind herself to always question the "y"s of life, and she wanted to be slightly different than the usual.

She has worn many hats and although some appear off-kilter, she's most proud of the hats labeled mother to Kellen and Caitlin, registered nurse in the Newborn Intensive Care Unit, sister, friend, Irish, and writer. Her sense of humor and love of laughter is her foundation of life. Karyn strives to share smiles and positive energy with the hope of making a difference in her small corner of the world.

Karyn can be seen with her cheap sunglasses on, ragtop down, music at blast level, and as the wind blows her hair in her eyes, visions of Pulitzers dance in her imagination. She also hopes to own a convertible one day.

Karyn has had Japanese forms of Senryu and kyoka poetry published in several online journals of Prune Juice. She is very proud to have her work included in two published anthologies of Japanese poetry — *Pieces of Her Mind: Women Find Their Voice in Centuries-Old Forms,* and *the Haiku Anthology: Observations and Insights in 2017.*

—KS

wine improves with age
when kept in a cool dark place
delayed perfection
if it's good enough for grapes
think I'll move to the basement
— Stockwell

when I was young
the world was so different
flashbacks
of the Grand Canyon when
it was called Slim-Jim Gully
— Stockwell

few people know
a jellyfish has no brain
freaky weird
it hasn't a heart either
just like my wacko ex-boyfriend
— Stockwell

the secret of youth
is not hidden magic
ask any kid
to share the wonder of childhood
hugs, laughter and chocolate
— Stockwell

mothers contain
an internal GPS
homing device with
pinpoint accuracy
"Mom. Where's my shoes…"
—**Stockwell**

Thanksgiving cook
hangs up her gravy-stained apron
the charge sounds
and she mutates into crazed
Black Friday stampeder
—**Stockwell**

~ • ~

one by one
I down each shot
wasted
I kneel before the porcelain god
and confess my sins
— **Barbour**

homesteaders
stake their claims and leave
cobwebs
I wonder where
the maid has gone
— **Barbour**

crows
gather on the housetops
revelations
an email announces
my exam results
— **Barbour**

teenagers
make out in the moonlight
lover's lane
on familiar ground old sweethearts
reignite yesterday's passion
— **Barbour**

Under the Ginkgo Tree

one hot and humid
day after another
summer doldrums
the betta fish watches me
watching it watch me
— **Barbour**

furrowed brows spoil
students' dreams of fun, frolic
standardized testing
teachers fret summer heat
awaiting their pass/fail score
— **Barbour**

~ . ~

rosemary lives
in Scarborough Fair
absurd
scents parley and sage
arc with thyme in a bottle
—Foor

Merlot and Riesling
met for a night cap
rosé at first sight
champagne says it must be true
she heard it through the grape vine
—Foor

blue denims
that fit you like a glove
pajama jeans
you can wear them
from the cradle to the grave
—Foor

my proctologist's
recommendation
internal exam
gives whole new meaning
to cavity search
—Foor

ampersand and tilde
got married in italics
period
hashtag, five caret diamond
plus or minus an iota
—Foor

heat wave
in the middle of winter
who knew
menopause could replace
my electric blanket
—Foor

aromatic bouquet
fills need you didn't know you had
red-hot
warms your bones from head to toe
powerful heat of my Ben-gay
—Foor

wedding cake
disappears at reception
bride's revenge
groom's canine ate the dessert
now he's doggone
—Foor

energizer bunny
hopped away from police
when arrested
he reluctantly pled guilty
and was charged with battery
—Foor

the hunter stops his car
on a winding country road
deer crossing sign
because everybody knows
the buck stops here
—Foor

golden retriever
wears his coat in winter
in summer
even when it's very hot
he wears his coat and pants
—Foor

love sick frog
sits alone on lily pad
ribbiting
until the object of his affection said
"I'm toad-ally into you"
—Foor

Under the Ginkgo Tree

thunder rumbles
across the blackened sky
heat lightning
flashes ghosts and gremlins
on the big screen
—**Foor**

vintner dreams
of moonshine and wine
collusion says
mix grapes with cowgirl
for a new brand of bootlegger
—**Foor**

kudzu covers
forest with vines
topiaries
of donkeys and elephants
for bi-partisan zoo
—**Foor**

~ · ~

red canna lilies
camouflage Granny's privy
eau de toilette
ladies are reassured as they
exit while primping their hair
—Griffin

full moon
casts light on Granny's front porch
night light
ensures we won't overstep
when we irrigate the grass
—Griffin

~ • ~

haiga (duality)
— by Ray Griffin

HAIKU

The origins of haiku, or hokku as it was called until the end of the 19th century, can be traced to the ancient renga dating back at least to 13th century Japan. It was not, however, until the 16th century that the renga's first three lines evolved into its own form, the haiku, and widely used in Japan. It was not until the early 20th century that haiku was first written in the English language. Ezra Pound has been credited as being the first to pen a haiku in English.

There has been much debate over the years about what haiku is and is not. This is particularly true relative the evolution of the modern haiku. Traditional haiku focuses on keen observations of nature or mankind and not imagined thoughts imposed upon it by the poet. The observation would be preceded or followed by a kireji, or enlightened insight. The haiku should contain a kigo, or seasonal reference, and be presented in a short / long / short format. The concept of the 5-7-5 syllable count evolved when haiku began to be written in English.

While the haiku guidelines and techniques are the same for nature, and mankind, the results can be amazingly and refreshingly different. Importantly, haiku themes in both groupings can be serious, religious, philosophical, and deeply thought provoking. However, it can also be light-hearted and humorous. Haiku normally have no title, and as with tanka, it can be both singular or plural.

The focus of this anthology is to write in traditional, not modern, haiku. The guidelines used to write traditional haiku and techniques are numerous and can often times be confusing. Guidelines that we used include the following: 1) using 17 syllables or less and presented in a short-long-short line format; 2) no personification of nature; 3) nonrhyming; 4) avoidance of excessive alliteration and overt metaphor and simile; 5) must capture an observable, moment-in-time, something that can be seen, felt, touched and/or smelled, and not a process-over-time; 6) should contain a kijo, or seasonal reference; 7) write in present tense, and avoid gerunds when possible; 8) the haiku should juxtaposition two concrete objects; not abstractions; 9) punctuation and capitalization should be used only when absolutely necessary; and 10) must have a moment of insight, or kireji. The kireji is the critical element where the poet brings the haiku together. It is not merely a description of the other two lines, but truly a moment of insight by use of techniques and insightful writing.

As Reichhold discusses in her previously referenced article, the haikuist can experiment with a number of techniques to help improve the overall quality of his/her haiku. These techniques include but are not limited to contrast, comparison, association, riddle, word play, sabi, wabi, and yugen, etc.

Haiku works extremely well with art and photography. When art and haiku are combined, it becomes known as haiga. It is important to embed the wording within the art/photograph in a non-obtrusive way. Both haiku and art must compliment, not compete with each other. Importantly, the haiku should not merely describe the artwork or photograph.

Finally, haiku should be about keen observation and insightfulness. Often times, it is left open, allowing for the reader to be engaged and to become part of the moment; in order to discover the kiregi on his/her own terms. Such is the magic, the beauty, of the haiku.

—**Ray Griffin**

hermit crab scurries
along shell-littered shore
prime real estate
— **Brixey**

in woodland clearing
exhausted stag sheds antlers
rut's over
— **Brixey**

sunlight dapples
leafy woodland glade
impressionist art
— **Brixey**

mountains loom
beyond my formal garden
borrowed scenery
— **Brixey**

nocturnal pride
king of the jungle
stirs
— **Brixey**

111

morning mist
shrouds abbey ruins
dove's coos echo
—**Brixey**

in stiff breeze
crimson leaves cling to branch
tenacious
—**Brixey**

vibrant colors
shimmer on wilderness lake
loon's plaintiff call
—**Brixey**

sun
viewed through moon gate
anomaly
—**Brixey**

shade
from copper beech tree
I daydream
—**Brixey**

112

A Word Picture

Ann Brixey

As far back as I can remember I have kept a journal. Writing about day to day happenings, things I had seen or heard. In junior school, my essays and compositions always got the highest marks. My teachers always praised my flair for writing. But there was one form that I was never successful at and that was writing poetry. Somehow rhyme and rhythm eluded me. As a dancer and singer, I knew about timing and rhythm, but for me, writing it simply did not work

Some years ago, I was delighted to come across haiku in a writing course. It was being taught as the more commonly recognized 5/7/5 syllable count poetry. I found it fun to write, I only had to worry about the number of syllables, but somehow something seemed to be missing, but I did not know what. Then I happened upon Alvin T. Ethington's courses on Japanese short form poetry. Suddenly, I discovered in the traditional forms of haiku and tanka that these were the perfect poetry forms for me.

I struggled in my early attempts, but Alvin's patience and understanding prompted me to work harder. Through his guidance I learned that *haiku* was an observation of a moment in time, not something imagined. He taught me how to capture that moment in a few words and how to make the reader see what I had seen.

Coupled with my love of photography, observing the world around me became a passion. From *haiku* and *tanka* it was a natural progression to expand my observations to *haibun* and *tanka* prose. Then Alvin introduced me to the world of *imperial court tanka*, this form truly appealed to my romantic side. I enjoyed writing messages between two fictitious lovers about their previous night's assignation. Making those notes subtly sensuous, without being blatant, certainly was a challenge. But it was in reading the comments of readers as they put their own interpretation these billet doux that fascinated me. It was then I realized that I had adopted the way the amorous pair would have written. Only the recipients would know the true meanings in the secret communications.

Alvin's teaching inspired me, along with the encouragement and help of my very good friends, Lois Funk, and Ray Griffin. These wonderful mentors have helped me to enjoy reading and writing Japanese Short Form Poetry. Each time I put pen to paper I am reminded of the words of my favorite English teacher, Sr. Louis Marie. "Paint a picture with your words. " This is what I try to do.

—AB

hedgehog
curls up in dried leaf pile
wispy smoke
— **Brixey**

snow monkeys
bath in hot springs
survival
— **Brixey**

wildflowers
grace old glass jar
my mother's smile
— **Brixey**

delicate blossoms
amongst hurricane debris
hardy
— **Brixey**

Blue Heron
scans deserted salt marsh
ebb tide
— **Brixey**

woodland
cloaked in autumn's mist
sound's muffled
— **Brixey**

amidst salt marsh grass
snowy egret looks skyward
contemplation
— **Brixey**

teenager
no longer smiles
peer pressure
— **Brixey**

grains of sand
trapped by beach grass
constant change
— **Brixey**

found on mountain's peak
fossilized sea creatures
ancient wonders
— **Brixey**

ducklings
reunited with mother
happy family
— **Brixey**

lynx watches
as raccoons cross grass land
opportunity missed
— **Brixey**

monarch butterflies
converge on familiar trees
kaleidoscope
— **Brixey**

twixt sea and river
a ribbon of golden sand
barrier isle
— **Brixey**

busy inlet
where river and ocean meet
windswept
— **Brixey**

as hillside snows melt
rivulets converge
waterfalls

haiga (as hillside snows melt)
– artwork by –Barbour
– haiku by – Brixey

wild berries
picked in August heat
best of the blues
— Foor

golden aspen leaves
shimmer in morning light
sunny side up
— Foor

monarch butterflies
emerge from chrysalis
the great escape
— Foor

house wrens
build nests in ivy wall
twitter nation
— Foor

hens and gobbler
emerge from morning fog
fan dance ensues
— Foor

coyotes howl
beneath blue moon's glow
opus
—**Foor**

brilliant yellow ginkgo
sways in autumn breeze
sublime
—**Foor**

cottontail rabbits
nibble cabbage plants
fast food
—**Foor**

snowflakes fall
on yesterday's flower bed
sleeping beauties
—**Foor**

brilliant star
shines over cow barn
silent night
—**Foor**

noisy Blue Jays
frighten Chickadees away
storm-troopers
— Foor

last rose of summer
blooms high on garden wall
therapy
— Foor

slowly
she walks to empty house
twilight
— Foor

puffy clouds
float on cerulean sky
paradisiacal
— Foor

lights go out
in daughter's playhouse
shattered dreams
— Foor

red tailed hawks
circles over meadow
field mice hide
— Foor

pale pink cloud bands
glow over the mountain top
art du jour
— Foor

twilight
filters into moss-covered glen
fairy's boudoir
— Foor

cattails
sway in morning breeze
heron heaven
— Foor

great horned owl
perched in massive oak
full moon rises
— Foor

starfish strewn
on black sandy beach
heavenly
—Griffin

Sage
enrichens evening meal
wise father
—Griffin

descended sun
ignites troposphere
fervent firmament
—Griffin

stalwart egret eyes
misty marshland habitat
adept purveyor
—Griffin

icicles
glisten in morning sunlight
prismatic delight
—Griffin

Under the Ginkgo Tree

snow-scape glistens
as morning sun alights ice crystals
a cardinal sings
—Griffin

Canada geese
aloft as first snow falls
escape artists
—Griffin

rain droplets
cling to barren limbs
translucent pearls
—Griffin

my dad's signature
in an old Fitzgerald book
connectivity
—Griffin

doe and fawn forage
for wild berries at wood's edge
dolce vita
—Griffin

Be True to Self

Ray Griffin

I have always enjoyed reading, and particularly so beautifully written prose that transports me to other places, and resplendent poetry that touches my heart and inspires me. Both serve to help me evolve beyond my self-imposed limitations. It is no wonder why Waugh, Wouk, Hardy, Lawrence, Hemingway, and Forster are among my favorite authors. And surely who could not be enamored with these poets: Shakespeare, Thomas, Bryon, Elizabeth Browning, Millay, Bashō, Frost, Oliver, and Price?

While I have never been able to wrap my mind around the concept of writing a novel, it was with poetry that I began to find my voice. My first ventures were in free verse of dubious value, but as my writing matured, as well as my understanding of the craft, my writing improved. I transitioned from free verse to form poetry.

The poetic forms in which I most enjoy writing include the Shakespearean sonnet, blank verse, and narrative. I also love writing in various Japanese short forms, particularly tanka and tanka prose. Some friends ask in which genre do I write, or how would I classify myself as a poet. It's a good question as my forms are rather fluid. I would say my writing focus is sometimes romantic, but not romance poetry. It is at times philosophical and other times introspective. Sometimes it is snarky — particularly when writing in senryu.

My muse is inspired by many things. Natural beauty never ceases to inspire, nor does interactions with friends and family, especially those whom I love. Sometimes I induce my muse to cooperate by bribing her with good red wine, a crackling fire, and/or music. If all three of these converge then I am surely going to write something!

Writing poetry allows me to express myself in ways I could not otherwise do. At times, the written word is easier to communicate than is the spoken word. Writing is a necessary part of my life, and on days when I do not have an opportunity to write, I feel diminished. Writing is to me what air is to fire.

I have learned that the best way to learn how to write, and to improve the craft of it, is to write each day, and to read from various authors and poets. Importantly, Caroline Brae, a close friend and Charlottesville poet, told me that a poet must be true to himself in order to write authentic, convincing poetry. In other words, in order to reach into the minds and touch the hearts of readers the poet and his poetry must be genuine. Otherwise, readers will see through his deception. I have found her words of wisdom to be true. Thus, my journey as a poet continues. It is my hope that one day I might reach the point where my verse inspires and touches the hearts of my readers.

—*RG*

colorful leaves
awhirl along trail's steep incline
Zephyrus
— **Griffin**

white flakes swirl
as I hike along creek's rocky path
snow globe
— **Griffin**

three owlets
nestled within limb's hollow
oracle
— **Griffin**

I write
of morning mist in my journal
a-mused
— **Griffin**

wind-blown leaves
swirl in upward spiral
pirouettes
— **Griffin**

Under the Ginkgo Tree

monarchs alight
on broad field of goldenrod
sovereigns redux
— **Griffin**

six deer dash
across the grassy bald
rush hour
— **Griffin**

yellow ginkgo aglow
in midst of Frasier furs
beacon
— **Griffin**

Parisian rooftops
shimmer in morning sun
potpourri
— **Griffin**

from creek's rounded rocks
we watch leaves float downstream
fall's regatta
— **Griffin**

~haiku~

sun emerges
from behind thunder clouds
peek-a-boo
—Johnson

spent blossoms
still hold great beauty
tomorrow's flowers
—Johnson

wet black nose
pressed against sun-warmed window
puppy love awaits
—Johnson

blackbirds converge
on frost-covered pines
flocked
—Johnson

hummingbird
amidst magnolia blossoms
morning's glory
—Johnson

129

Under the Ginkgo Tree

wild turkey
soars across the road
Thanksgiving flight
—**Johnson**

atop thick stems
curved leaves collect raindrops
nature's teacup
—**Johnson**

beaver dam
across a languid stream
meadow's birth
—**Johnson**

bird's nest
coated with heavy frost
avian igloo
—**Johnson**

country roads
topped with scalloped snow drifts
undulating
—**Johnson**

snowflakes
land on chestnut mare
equine dandruff
—Johnson

crisp multi-hued leaves
rustle in cool breeze
autumn concert
—Johnson

orange, red, golden
leaves strewn across dormant ground
fall's blazing garland
—Johnson

hungry horse
nibbles on hay bale
shredded wheat
—Johnson

lone pink water lily
adorns farm pond
exquisite jewelry
—Johnson

Under the Ginkgo Tree

white sky
over snow-drifted road
lost horizon
—Johnson

~ • ~

glasswing butterfly
flits with fragile translucence
rainforest window
—Stockwell

robins gather
for early morning breakfast
lawn party
—Stockwell

empty swing
sways in autumn breeze
school begins
—Stockwell

sunrise reveals
glitter of night's snowfall
shoveling diamonds
— Stockwell

butterflies gather
in field of flowers at sunrise
breakfast club
— Stockwell

crumpled oak leaves
cover sleeping flower garden
sweater weather
— Stockwell

dandelions
crushed by tiny hands
child's bouquet
— Stockwell

fragrant magnolia
fills air with spring sweetness
memories of home
— Stockwell

ginkgo leaves
flutter in July breeze
minature fans

haiga (ginkgo leaves)
— artwork by pixabay.com
— haiku by Karyn Stockwell

garden strawberries
gathered in red-stained apron
Grandma's jelly
— Stockwell

lone timber wolf
wails under hunter's moon
dog house empty
— Stockwell

morning birds
announce summer's arrival
hallelujah choir
— Stockwell

one dim star
lost among millions
hope shines through
— Stockwell

rain puddles
at kids' school bus stop
group mud shower
— Stockwell

solitary star
streaks across night sky
unanswered wish
—Stockwell

snowflakes
sculpt intricate design
lace doily
—Stockwell

spring rain drips
from graveside tent
my bones ache
—Stockwell

swans missing
as pond freezes overnight
my lunch goes unshared
—Stockwell

Venus flytrap
lures unwary prey
ambush
—Stockwell

wind scatters
countless dandelion seeds
feathered umbrellas
— Stockwell

garden rose
sparkles with dewdrops
morning devotion
— Stockwell

ocean tide pool
captures luminous sea star
I make a wish
— Stockwell

tree frog's eggs hatch
on forest leaf over pond
tadpole's waterslide
— Stockwell

newborn turtles
scamper from sand to sea
instinctive journey
— Stockwell

caesura
the dragonfly lingers
on a twig
—**Barbour**

ebb tide
the moonlight drifts
out to sea
—**Barbour**

crescendo
a chorus of spring peepers
at twilight
—**Barbour**

quietude
the sea swallows
ship's wake
—**Barbour**

a bouquet
of Queen Ann's Lace for mom
mea culpa
—**Barbour**

ripples
distant thunder
echoes

haiga (ripples)
— artwork by Diana Barbour
— haiku by Ann Brixey

139

congregation
bows head in silent prayer
white daffodils
—**Barbour**

sunrise
breaks through the cloud cover
mood swings
—**Barbour**

crocuses bloom
all over the graveyard
resurrection
—**Barbour**

an old man
traces names on the wall
Veteran's Day
—**Barbour**

dewdrops
a spider's web captures
the sunrise
—**Barbour**

pollen
coats my car in yellow
nature's spray paint
— **Barbour**

crystal tree branches
tinkle sweetly in the wind
winter lullaby
— **Barbour**

melted butter
drips from the cob down my chin
satisfaction
— **Barbour**

ocean waves
roll up the beach
sea stories
— **Barbour**

~ • ~

brilliant sunset
absorbs all that approaches
portal

color strata
change continuously
kaleidoscope

only the wind
pierces the silence
awed

haiku suite art (awed)
– by Ray Griffin

HAIKU SUITE

The traditional haiku suite follows the same guidelines as provided in the previous section for traditional haiku. With that said, haiku grouped together in a suite allow the poet to develop a more detailed story. Importantly, each haiku in a suite must be aligned and work together. Additionally, each haiku must also be able to stand on its own.

For the superstitious, the poet would want to avoid a haiku suite with only four or nine haiku. These are bad luck numbers in Japan. Good luck numbers would be seven and eight.

—Ray Griffin

haiku suite (peafowl)

peafowl
lifts and fans his covert feathers
cocksure

strutting peacocks
fan, strut and call to peahens
eyes all seeing

peahen
responds to peacock's fan
one-nighter
—Griffin

143

Under the Ginkgo Tree

haiku suite (spring)

sun-struck daffodils
bloom on craggy mountainside
tranquil spring morning

creeping pink phlox
cascade over garden wall
frosted rockery

grape hyacinths grow
beneath the blooming lilac tree
royal flush

candy cotton tulips
stand row after row
pastel pleasures

lichens flourish
on moss-covered river birch
embellishments

storm clouds
build in azure sky
April showers
—**Foor**

It's Never too Late

Janet Foor

I was always creative, but creative writing was not part of my life. I'm sure I wrote for school but only when necessary. I had writing requirements for work that were necessary.

In the years I worked in emergency management, I wrote countless reports including employee evaluations and after-action reports for nuclear power plant drills and exercises. Sometimes, you must take a negative and turn it into a positive even when there is little positive to be found. I guess you could say that I learned to write creatively while working for the government. I feel that those years of work-related writing gave me the confidence for what was to come.

Fast forward many years to my retirement. (hold on – not that many years!) We moved to North Carolina where I made new friends and we decided to read a book together. "The Artist Way" by Julia Cameron. The reader is asked to write three, long hand notebook pages every day that Julia calls "morning pages". That seemed daunting at first, but within a few weeks, I was looking forward to writing them. The morning pages are a stream of consciousness writing every morning.

One day, following my morning pages, I composed a poem which I shared with my friends. Their encouragement inspired me to continue to write. I expanded my writing to short stories and various poetic forms. I enjoy wordsmithing and finding the right word to complete a thought or theme. Mark Twain said, "The difference between the *almost right* word and the *right* word is really a large matter. 'tis the difference between the lightning bug and the lightning." That thought has always stayed with me.

I found a website, *FanStory*, where I could post my poems and take writing classes. The poets and writers on this site critique each other's work as they continue to learn and write. I believe that our creativity is a gift from God and when we use our creativity, it is our gift to God.

A few years ago, a friend and fellow poet, Ray Griffin, introduced me to Japanese short form poetry. This brought a new challenge. I joined a group of poets who are encouraging as well. They have taught and inspired me to continue this journey.

I'm still writing morning pages and have read other Julia Cameron books like, "It's Never Too Late to Begin Again" and you know what, it really is never too late. That along with my husband, who is my best critic and biggest fan, I don't know how I missed this creative adventure of writing for so long.

—JF

haiku suite (summer)

waterfall
spills into iridescent brook
fisherman's dream

crystal raindrops
glisten in summer heat
liquid sunshine

quetzal green stream
meanders through meadow
catfish jump

sapphire colored river
flows into old millpond
priceless jewel

droplets fall
into Lake Minnetonka
purple rain

rainbow
appears in opalescent sky
promise
  —Foor

147

luscious valleys
dip between rugged ridges
sanctuary

haiga (luscious valleys)
— photograph by Sherrie Hygon
— by Janet Foor

haiku suite (gentle rain)

gentle rain
sifts through oak's leaves
muse aroused

muse aroused
on cool, damp summer night
sounds converge

sounds converge
beneath Lyra's twinkling lights
kaleidoscope

kaleidoscope
of Summer Triangle's stars
night sky alights

night sky alights
impatiens along serpentine wall
life's chosen path

life's chosen path
unfolds on foxed parchment
sepia ink

sepia ink
reveals innermost self
gentle rain
            —Griffin

Under the Ginkgo Tree

haiku suite (bluebird)

lone bluebird
calls out from berry branch
musical solo

male bluebird
serenades on flowered bough
duet begins

mother bluebird
edges fledglings from nest
flight training

royal bluebird pair
perch on throne of spring flowers
morning songfest reigns

bluebirds gather
around family nest
home tweet home
—Stockwell

haiku suite (zoogenic)

hippo
relaxes in mud bath
spa treatment

giraffe
strolls along walkway
high fashion show

chimp
entertains with antics
monkey business
— **Stockwell**

Under the Ginkgo Tree

haiku suite (silent spectre)

silent spectre
glides through woodland canopy
mysterious

ariel hunter
in nighttime's darkened skies
formidable

field mice
strip ripened wheat sheafs
unconcerned

greenish eyes
amongst cornfield's stubble
night-time prowler

moon hidden
snowy owl
blinks
— **Brixey**

haiku suite (sun-dappled path)

sun-dappled path
through leafy wooded glade
tranquility

waterlilies'
reflections on still pond
elusive beauty

broad flat leaves
provide haven for koi
heron waits

dragonfly hovers
above lotus blossom
whirligig

ripples radiate
as beetles skim surface
turmoil
—**Brixey**

Under the Ginkgo Tree

haiku suite (the blues)

dawn arrives
on water colored sky
impressionistic

indigo bunting
lands on my garden wall
surprise

chicory and milkweed
align old country roads
monarch heaven

wild larkspur
paint hillside a lovely hue
enchantment

huckleberries for breakfast
delightful treat to start my day
pass the sugar please
—Foor

haiku suite (I'm home)

new moon rises
over misty blue mountains
silver light

campfire crackles
until embers are red-hot
wiener roast

barn owl
swoops low in search of food
dinner time

crickets' chirps
resonate under porch steps
nocturnal opus

stars wink
through indigo sky
serenity
—Foor

late summer's soft light
casts long shadows across vineyard
muse beckons

haiga (late summer's soft light)
– photo by Elizabeth Smith
– haiku by Ray Griffin

haiku suite (through vineyard's fields)

worn path
meanders through vineyard's fields
wind's whispers

wafting fog veils
ascendant crescent moon
evanescence

late afternoon's chill
draws us closer to fire pit's warmth
twilight's embrace

embers glow
as we sip Sangiovese
sated

I gaze
into your hazel eyes
il mio amore
--Griffin

Under the Ginkgo Tree

haiku suite (sky works)

sunset display
melds with magenta light
kaleidoscope

orange orb descends
sapphire horizon
transitions

full moon ascends
over ancient oak
silhouetted sentinel

illumination
casts elongated shadows
eerie canvas

dawn's light
dims Luna's brilliance
new day's birth

brilliant sunlight
cast through azure skies
ancient oak glows
— Stockwell

haiku suite (autumn corn)

golden corn stalks
crackle in autumn wind
brittle knees

mid-western farmer
creates intricate corn maze
dead-end puzzle

harvester gathers
acres of dried corn crop
scarecrow hangs head
— Stockwell

Under the Ginkgo Tree

haiku suite (funeral)

September rain
mingles with grief-stricken tears
rainbow of umbrellas

bagpiper honors
fallen soldier at gravesite
"Going Home"

family gathers
under oak tree for service
goldfish funeral
—Stockwell

haiku suite (samurai)

young boy
accepts samurai's curved sword
dedication

at height of beauty
cherry blossom falls
samurai bows

samurai
shows no sign of weakness
his badge of honor
—**Brixey**

...*The blistering, sultry sun hangs low when we arrive. The surface is almost as still as Monet's "Water Lilies-Setting Sun"*...

a ripple unfolds
across cool placid lake
Bob's lure

haibun art (the bait)
— photo by Robert Pridgen
— tanka prose by — Ray Griffin

HAIBUN

Haibun is a challenging form of Japanese poetry that was first written during the 17th century. Originally written as travel journal entries, the form currently includes autobiographies, life experiences, essays, diary entries, and short sketches of love, events, objects, or places. Haibun is now a worldwide established genre which has gained significant popularity in recent years.

The most important aspects of a haibun are its title, prose, and haiku. Each should be separate and able to stand on their own, but they must also be inter-connected. They should mirror each other without duplication. Haibun can be written in under 100 words or can go into the hundreds. Generally speaking, shorter length is preferred.

- TITLE — gives a clue to what will follow. Most expert writers state the title should be different from anything stated in the prose or poem. In other words, the title is the lure to capture the reader's interest.

- PROSE — should tell of a single event, often, something personal, written in present tense like it's happening now. Many references state haibun should contain a mixture of regular sentences along with short sentences. Incomplete and terse sentence fragments are encouraged. An important aspect of haibun prose is specifically conveying to the reader what the writer is trying to communicate, be it an image, emotion, life lesson, or a connection to people or nature that others can relate. Many haibun writers use as few articles as possible and try to avoid adverbs and overuse of gerunds. As with haiku and tanka, word efficiency and word effectiveness is critical to successful haibun writing.

163

- HAIKU — must relate to topic of prose, but maintain the guidelines of haiku. It should be 17 syllables, or less, written in present tense, have two lines of concrete imagery which are grammatically connected, an ah-ha line (satori) which allows the reader to think beyond the words, no capitalization except for proper names, punctuation avoided, no rhymes, and use of a kigo or seasonal word is encouraged in haiku. Most writers try to use only needed words, so articles and adverbs are avoided. Also, gerunds and -ing words should not be used if possible.

Haibun is an exciting and creative experience in expression. The beauty and challenge of the form's combination of sensory observation, expressed in prose and poetry, is truly a unique and rewarding format in which to write and read.

—**Karyn Stockwell**

haibun (outburst)

It starts with a faint sound of rumbling. The sky gets murky with dark clouds. Day becomes night. I light a candle. Strong wind whips oak branches that slap against the house. Lightning flashes increase. One-one thousand... two-one thousand... three-one thousand. Three miles before it gets to me. I sit on the bay window seat with my scaredy-cat dog, Jaxson, on my lap. Drops of rain splash against the glass like a bucket being tossed against the pane. One-one thousand... two-one thousand. Lightning illuminates the tire swing jerking back and forth with a ghost rider.

The light show mesmerizes me. Wind and rain knockabout the flowers. One-one... Crash! Jaxson and I jump with the sudden thunderclap. We settle back down, and the wind rushes the clouds along. Mom would cuddle me during such a ruckus. Never being scared, I'd pretend. I always thought she was the one more scared. I'd feel safe and protected with her warm embrace. My dog and I snuggle. The sky lightens up and the strikes of lightning and claps of thunder lessen. Too soon, it's gone.

summer storm
crashes in with force
drum solo
— Stockwell

Under the Ginkgo Tree

haibun (goin' for broke)

I walk into the casino with money in my pocket. Cha-ching smiles and welcome back sneers greet me. Flashing neon lures me deeper into the isolation of obsession. Symphony of clinks and clanks drown out cries of desperation. One-more-time urgency on faces spending rent money. Old lady in wheelchair. Chain smokers pushing penny slot buttons. Young stud swaggers to blackjack table with glass of Jack for support. Long line of losers wait their turn at the ATM and stare at the short line of winners cashing in. Games of chance with no probabilities. No windfall. No easy money. No good fortune bestowed by white marbles on a black and red wheel. Russian roulette spins player into no pay-out hell. I walk out of the casino with money never leaving my pocket. Jackpot.

four-leaf clover
symbolizes good luck
serendipity
— Stockwell

My Life's Passion

Karyn Stockwell

Writing is like breathing to me. It is a vital part of who I am, and I can't imagine a single day without digging into my imagination to capture the ideas waiting to be written in the form of prose or poetry. It's a passion I never want to surrender.

The process of writing gives me a vast opportunity to convey, in any format I desire, what I feel at any given moment about any topic I choose. I've dabbled in non-fiction and explored mystery and crime stories, sports-related tales, and horror and thriller prose. I've had a go with a variety of poetic formats, romance, and even some mature stories. But I've found myself embracing and loving the short forms of prose—flash fiction, and poetry—Japanese short forms.

Being able to write in the Japanese short poetry forms is such a rewarding and exciting experience for me. The forms embrace people, nature, humor, emotions, and insight into life. These poetry forms are centuries old, and I'm truly proud and thrilled to share my poems with readers familiar and those newly discovering these amazing forms. I love to take one moment of observation and convey that awareness with sensory imagery and share with readers an opportunity to feel they have experienced the observed moment with me. There's so much in life to celebrate, and the many forms of Japanese poetry gives me the chance to praise and honor the beauty and wonder of life.

I often like to include humor in my writings. Everyone needs more opportunities to laugh these days. So often, we're consumed by the activities of life, and we overlook the funny things people do or say, and we miss all the

167

humorous possibilities in our lives from people, animals, and nature. Japanese forms of senryu, kyoka, haibun, and even haiku give me a way to express the humor and irony of life. Laughter is contagious. Who doesn't need more moments when the seriousness and trials of life can be set aside and forgotten while we smile, chuckle, giggle, or laugh at ourselves and life.

Often, writing flows like some unseen keyboardist has taken over my fingers. I've come to love and depend on the poet in my soul, who can say with brevity what a million prose words couldn't possibly convey. I love writing both prose and poetry, but I want to continue learning how the magic of Japanese short forms can bring out the best in me as an observer of life and share that magic in my poetry.

Writing isn't about making money, getting famous, getting dates, getting laid, or making friends. In the end, it's about enriching the lives of those who will read your work, and enriching your own life, as well.
— *Stephen King*

—KS

haibun (holding pattern)

Chicago's Northwestern Hospital Emergency Room. Crowded like a crammed rush hour El train. Every waiting room chair filled. They wait. Young mother-to-be practices hee-hoo-hee-hoo breathing. A string of deep hacking coughs from a man who doesn't cover his mouth. Child cries. Old woman rocks and sings *Stardust*. A family weeps and clutches each other as chaplain escorts them away. Man in a grimy coat and Sox cap refills Styrofoam cup with free coffee. Teenager with bloodied bandana around his thigh texts on cell. Old man in the corner moans.

Receptionist makes sure all paperwork's in order. Proof of insurance, patient rights, health history, HIPPAA privacy form. Triage nurse prioritizes injuries and illnesses. She controls the lottery numbers. Ambulance arrives and paramedics rush through door with stretcher. Lottery numbers pushed back. Overhead speaker calls Code Blue for ER room seven. They wait. Man coughs and spreads germs. Child screams. Woman rocks and sings *Mack the Knife*. Coffee man empties pot and switches it off. Teenager never looks up from his iPhone. They wait. Patients without names. Nurse with clipboard calls out, "Rebecca?" Pregnant lady goes forward, eases into wheelchair and is whisked away to baby land. Old man stops moaning and slumps. No one notices he's not breathing. Hours later, no one responds to the clipboard nurse's call: "Joseph?"

lone flower
in garden perishes
final gasp
— Stockwell

169

Under the Ginkgo Tree

haibun (one more chore)

nor'easter
the sound of silence
in the wind

Walking through the backdoor of the farmhouse, I drop the slop bucket into the deep sink. The farmer's widow, Mrs. J, asks me to check on the far field and do whatever needs to be done. At the barn, the horses and the cows mill about, waiting. I check the water trough, break up the ice, put out a fresh salt block, and then grab the closest bale of hay, pulling hard. Stuck. I yank, push, kick, stomp, pull again, curse... An animal suddenly snorts and grunts. In the opening opposite me stands the bull, black, huge, his tail switching back and forth, his breath visible with each exhale

Mexican standoff
falling snow deadens the noise
of knocking knees
— **Barbour**

amazon.com®

SX7mhXh2rh

Your order of December 21, 2022 (Order ID 114-9097394-3574622)

Qty.	Item	Item Price	Total
1	Under the Ginkgo Tree: An Anthology of Traditional Japanese Short Form Poetry Griffin, Ray --- Paperback **1792851936** 1792851936 9781792851933	$14.99	$14.99
		Subtotal	$14.99
		Order Total	$14.99
		Paid via credit/debit	$14.99

This shipment completes your order.

B3-M2

Return or replace your item
Visit Amazon.com/returns

0/X7mhXh2rh/-1 of 1-//EUG5-DAY/second/0/1223-11:30/1222-21:26

an

haibun (wash down)

Saturday. Third day of vacation. The red lights of the alarm clock stab my eyes. 6:00 AM! Fifteen years a civilian and I still wake at reveille. Time to start that long to-do list. Through the open bedroom window, the damp, gray dawn creeps in. The absence of bird song, disquieting, depressing, yet that old Navy training drives me to get going. I move to get up. The sleeping cat at the end of my bed rolls over, curling himself tighter around my foot. He purrs. I feel the vibrations. So soothing. Perhaps the cat has the right idea. Falling into the pillow, unconsciousness quickly takes me back to sleep.

low tide
the trash men take away
pieces of my life
— **Barbour**

haibun (lull before the storm)

Daybreak. A faint glow on the dark horizon indicates sunrise. Despite a hurricane warning, the ocean is strangely calm. The deep gray green surface ripples like silk. On a ribbon of inky black, several bulky vessels loom. Outlines stark against the ominous gray cloud backdrop. At the shoreline, a great blue heron waits patiently for some unsuspecting fish to swim by. Sanderlings brave the incoming tide. Frenzied probing in wet sand. Small brown crabs scuttle to find safe hideaways. Heron turns his head. Concentration is lost. The scurrying intruders are carefully inspected. Then, with neck extended, he flies off to find a more secluded haven farther up the beach.

tidal breakers
footprints disappear
from shell-littered sand
— **Brixey**

haibun (northwoods)

Our snowshoes leave a trail in the powdery snow. We reach the river bank. Stop, take a deep breath. Biting cold burns our nostrils. Ahead, across a bridge of ice, unfamiliar territory - the forest. Tree tops are illuminated in the light of a ghostly moon. Soon thick clouds roll in. Darkness. Solitude. Somewhere in the distance a wolf howls and is quickly answered. Then, silence. Snow begins to fall, gently. With childlike glee we shake off our mittens to catch the first flakes on bare hands.

aural display
in sapphire skies
polar night
—Brixey

haibun (seascape)

Gnarly driftwood pieces sit abandoned on the small sandbar. A perfect spot to watch the sun set over Kachemak Bay. A cold wind blows. Seabirds squawk and circle overhead. Splash! The kittiwakes dive after bait fish. Snow geese skim the frigid water. I stop and listen. Over the water, I hear the humpback whales' song. Delighted, I gaze at the creamy yellow ribbons of light glow over the distant mountains. Waves lap the shore and recede with the outgoing tide. Seashells and red algae are exposed on the sand. Shivering, I pull my red muffler tight as gusts whip the sea.

chilled-to-the-bone
I retreat to my cabin
hot chocolate time
—**Foor**

haibun (preparation)

It's early October. The weather is changing. From my front porch, I watch the ruby-throated humming-birds stock up on nectar for their epic migration. Their energy is incredible. They swoop from feeder to feeder and back again. The last red cannas of summer are next on their menu. Squirrels scurry. They gather acorns for their winter fare. Glorious leaves of red and gold drift past me and clutter the ground. Out of the corner of my eye I see a wondrous sight. Five, no six, beautiful monarch butterflies. They flit from bush to flower and back again. I watch in amazement. Orange and black wings flutter in the gentle breeze. Overhead, Canadian geese honk announcing their departure. Their V-shaped formation fades and disappears over the horizon.

> I place warm quilt
> at the foot of my bed
> Grandma's art.
> —**Foor**

haibun (the bait)

Some days it's just best to stay in bed and lie beneath the ceiling fan's warbling breeze. Damn air conditioning went out during the night. Eighty-three degrees at dawn. Morning air is sultry, heavy and butter-thick with dripping Southern humidity. Murky-grey skies scream air pollution. No wind. No fluttering of leaves. Mid-day sun bears down like a sweaty whore on Saturday night. Work is like being chained to Dante's furnace. I'm frayed and enervated to the point of rigor mortis from all of the day's BS. A friend calls: "Let's do Kerr and a six-pack of brew."
"Hell yeah!" I reply.

The red-orange sun hangs low in the sky when we arrive. The water's surface is as still as Monet's *Water Lilies-Setting Sun.* Surreal. Sublime. We dangle our feet in the clear, softly lapping shallow water. Refreshed. We gulp down a couple of beers. The twain meets as orb's fiery glow melds with lake's undulating rim. Cool. Relaxed. I'm not miserable anymore. Uninhibited, I breathe in deeply and cast my eyes towards distant fishing boat. I toss my jeans towards shore before diving into lake's coolness...

a ripple unfolds
across cool placid lake
Bob's lure
— Griffin

haibun (resplendence)

I awake at 04:00. Well before twilight's magenta blush crests Afton ridge. I toss and turn. Restless. Fitful. Full moon's glow casts shadows on the courtyard beneath my window. My mind is wide awake! My body aches for rest. Why must old men awake to make nightly trips to the loo? Dawn's soft light evolves the night sky. Birdsong begins to fill the air. I lumber down the stairs to brew a pot of Columbian. The beans' aroma sends me over the edge. Amaretto enhanced. I sip robust java and savor a strip of thick-sliced bacon.

I settle down in my patio chair. The morning coolness invites me to relax and enjoy nature. Quietly, a buck appears in the thicket. Quirky. He's alert to morning sounds. Smells. I breathe calmly. Silently. Observant. The buck affirms his domain. He gazes, then grazes. A doe appears…

deer forage
at dawn's early light
Monet paints
— Griffin

naiads preside
over secluded pond
ripple effect

haiga (naiads preside)
– by Ann Brixey

haibun (floating sparks)

Almost dusk. Seneca Street kids meet at the designated spot in the small neighborhood park. We bring our Welch's jelly, Peter Pan peanut butter, or Mason canning jars with holes poked in the lids. We wait. On the lookout to spot evening's first lightning bugs. "There's one!" Jimmy Santora hollers. "There's another! Wow, look at 'em all!" And off we scatter to chase the glittering beetles. I stand still by an oak tree, and behold with delight the tiny lights blinking off and on. I grab one mid-air. Trap another by my feet with the glass

Taking our tiny marvels, the friends form a circle on the ground. We show off our collections. Lift the flickering jars to light-up the goofy faces we make. Form air circles like 4th of July sparklers. Shine them like small nature's flashlights. Walter's Mom yells for him to come home. Annie's Mom signals with their porch light. Kevin Connors counts to three. Together we remove the lids and set them free like a burst of exploding stars. Winking and sparkling in the darkening sky. They head on home. So do we. At the edge of the park. I turn and stare at the beauty, enchanted by their dazzling magic. The glittering glow transforms a city park into a twinkling fairy woods.

fireflies
perform their summer dance
jitterbug light show
— Stockwell

Under the Ginkgo Tree

haibun (individuality)

I'm six. Staring into the garish light of the bathroom mirror. The reflection screams: I don't look anything like Annie Wilson. She's the prettiest girl in first grade. Boys love her. Teacher's pet. Fancy girly dresses with frilly socks and black patent leather shoes. Straight A's. Big brown eyes, perfect nose and mouth. The best part is her brunette hair. She just got the latest haircut everyone wants — the bubble cut. Just like my new Barbie doll. Every girl wants hair like Annie's. Jealousy starts early. Self-image and self-esteem work their way into a young girl's perception.

I beg my parents to get my hair cut. I want to look like Annie. Dad shakes his head and takes me to the mirror. "You don't want to be her, honey. Look at your beautiful blue eyes. Your cute little freckles on your perfect face. Your blonde hair makes you look like Cinderella." I look at him instead of the reflection. He tugs on my ponytail. "Annie's hair is too short to tie back. No more pretty ribbons. Being yourself, princess, makes you beautiful. Now, you're the prettiest girl in the first grade." I believe him.

peacock
displays iridescent plumage
struts confidence
— Stockwell

haibun (taking off)

Country girl in the big city. Lonely for home. Missing family. Afraid, but proud of her independence. Standing on the corner in the rain, Annamarie waits for the streetlight to flash permission to walk. Taxi zooms through the crosswalk puddle. It splashes dirty street water on her shoes, legs, and skirt. The trolley bus, getting electrical power from the overhead lines, snaps and pops with each spark. Bus advertises upcoming Paul McCartney concert at Seattle's Key Arena. Drivers lay on their horns if vehicles ahead don't move in a second. Tires splash through the wet pavement. Sirens blare from passing ambulance and police car. Spring rain is chilly as it drips off her hood onto her face.

A job interview waits across the street. Streetlight changes, but she doesn't move off the corner. Torn between self-reliance and the security of home. Her mind races. Stay in Seattle? Or home? Interview or bus station? The sign flashes. Annamarie makes her decision to fly.

flight school
gives lessons to nestlings
mother robin
— **Stockwell**

haibun (bridges)

4 P.M. The clinic's receptionist asks me to wait. A few minutes later, a technician leads me to an empty room. The odor of the cleaning antiseptic is strong. A second technician brings my cat in. He's frail and his breathing labored. I take him. He nuzzles me, purring softly.

"There's nothing more I can do. The infection, his allergies... It's just too much for the old boy..."
"Is he suffering?"
"Yes, I think so..."

The tears rolling down my face tell the doctor what to do. In my arms, Yoda, my beloved friend of eight years, crosses over.

crepuscular rays
in the midst of upheaval
momentary peace
—**Barbour**

Creativity

Diana Barbour

Writing for me is an arduous task. The word task is putting it lightly, to say the least. Through elementary, middle and high school, and even into university I have struggled with the writing process. I am the quintessential bi-polar writer. During manic periods, output is high and oddly enough the response to said output is favorable and encouraging. During depressed periods output is low and response to that output discouraging. Writer's block is a constant battle.

The problem is not the creativity, the idea, but rather the nouns and verbs necessary to convey the vision I see so that another may enjoy it as well. Too often, the vision, great and wonderful, is lost as soon as the pencil touches the paper, or the fingers strike the keyboard. Rewrites are lessons in surviving frustration. I have not yet discovered a cure for this. Writing, therefore, has become a journey in which the destination and the even the route taken to get there are unknown to me until the poem or piece of prose is finished and brings pleasure to another.

I have been dabbling in writing poetry and prose since second grade. It was then that I developed a love for poetry or at least willingness to read it and find pleasure in it. As a child I imitated that which I liked. In time, simple rhymes gave way to free verse and eventually short prose. Japanese short form poetry has become my favorite and the poetic forms I prefer to write. It is their simplicity that I find alluring. But I do not call myself a writer, a poet, or a haijin because I am still on that long journey; one just begun.

I can offer no one insight into how to write or advice on how to become a writer or poet. All I say is that if writing of any kind is what one wishes to pursue then one must do it every day and stick to it through all the highs and lows.

—DB

haibun (dog days)

Betta in a bowl, a hexagon, swims round and round, darting from side to side, over and under the ruin and through the plants. In the corners he wiggles and puffs up, big, bad, scary… Dropping in some food pellets, he attacks the surface, a feeding frenzy. Watching, I hum the theme from *Jaws.* Nothing left. Sudden stillness, full fish float, slowly rising and falling, fins fanned out, red, white, blue… Beautiful. Moving again, he restarts his routine.

thunder clap
the summer monotony
concludes
—Barbour

haibun (culture shock)

Chicago. Barnes and Noble parking lot. I wait in the summer sun. A car horn honks. The young woman waves and parks. It's Judith. I haven't seen her in years. We run toward each other, meeting in the middle. We shower each other with air kisses and collapse into a bear hug. Arm-in-arm we walk to the store. At the entrance, we hear a boy say loudly, "Mommy, are those two girls lesbians?"

a ladybug
settles in my palm
first impressions
— **Barbour**

Under the Ginkgo Tree

haibun (morning serenade)

On the gentle hillside, dew-soaked ferns, heather and gorse perfume the air. A bumblebee thrums lazily, flying from blossom to blossom in search of nectar. In the branches of the tall stately pines, birds chirp happily. Nesting season is in full swing. A whir of wings. A pair of grouse leaves the cover of the heather. From a thicket a cuckoo calls longingly. Overhead, a hawk soars. before swooping down. A distant plaintive bleat. An anxious ewe answers. Excited barks from the farmyard. An engine's roar joins the cacophony of a nearby rookery. A tractor heads out. Today's business has started

on grassy slopes
lambs gambol
wily fox
— **Brixey**

haibun (workday's done)

Anxious to reach the well-lit road I tread carefully. This tortuous, but unlit lane, with its high stone wall on one side and fenced in hedges on the other, provides a quicker route. Tonight the wind whips the sleet. It not only stings my face but makes the cobbled stones treacherous to walk on. Note to self, no more wearing high heeled shoes in winter. My shopping basket loaded with Christmas gifts and wine, starts to feel heavy. Stop for a moment. Switch hands. Much better. Almost at the bottom of the hill. A tug. Someone yanks on my bag. Terror. No point in screams they won't be heard. A slow-motion turn to face my attacker. No-one is there. Feeling foolish I realize what has happened. Changing hands had re-positioned my goodies everything was slipping backward. Phew! Readjustments made, I swallow hard and hurry on. The main road at last. There is a bus rounding the corner. Hurry! I can be at the bus stop before it.

slushy road
freezes overnight
ice-slide
— Brixey

187

Under the Ginkgo Tree

haibun (rendezvous)

Barefoot, I hurry down the stone covered path to the lake. Moonlight made the wet pebbles glow beneath my feet. Ouch! I stepped on a sharp twig on the trail. Jumping up and down, I stub my toe. Gripping a tree branch to regain my balance, it snaps in two. A startled doe and her fawn quickly run off into the forest. Finally, the water's edge is in sight. I step carefully into the glimmering starlit pool. Softly you whisper my name, and I surrender to your touch.

A screech owl swoops overhead in search of his dinner. Only his wise eyes see our midnight tryst.

lovers meet
under canopy of night
fifty shades of gray
— **Foor**

haibun (life is good)

   Children's laughter is heard from the shore. Rafters float the French Broad River.   Meandering goose and her brood of downy goslings' dive for minnows.   Red-tailed hawks circle overhead. Gnats don't escape swallows skimming the water's surface. Songbirds chirp. Ducks quack. Squirrels scurry up a giant tulip tree. Weeping willows sway in the soft summer breeze.   Leaves gently brushing the river's edge. Chrystal clear water gurgles over mossy rocks. A ring of waves reverberates from an angler's lure. In the distance, a banjo plays a toe-tapping bluegrass tune.

small mouth bass
jumps for blue-winged dragonfly
catch-of-the-day
—Foor

Under the Ginkgo Tree

haibun (balance)

Ascending Afton's eastern slope caused me pause. I'm behind seven transfer trucks trying to make it up the steep incline. Slow and slower trying to compete for leadership of the creeping and crawling vehicles. The rest of us are stuck in a slow-as-molasses traffic jam. How could it take 30 minutes to drive six miles on a road posted at 70? I'm tense. I turn up the music and cut down the air conditioning.

I sigh a breath of relief as I pull into my driveway 50 minutes later. I disembark from my car. All I could think of was a good cold one from which to gulp, initially, and then sip. I calm down from the tedious journey. Yes! There's Ms. Artois in the fridge. Left door panel. I place the baby's lips against my heated forehead. Relief! The taste of her is sweeter than anything I've tasted all day long. I settle into my old wicker chair on the patio under ancient oak's shadow. I love this tree! Soothing. Entrancing. Within five minutes I'm cooled and relaxed from Stella's kiss, the sifting breezes through the trees, and wonderful, luscious, cooling shade.

late June's heat
dissipates beneath my ancient oak
equilibrium
—Griffin

haibun (virga)

It's 07:00 and uncomfortably warm for this time of day. No breezes. Though the sun is still low, it's torridity sears my face as I start my morning walk. I know I'm crazy to walk 10 kilometers in this heat. But I am stubborn as hell. I need the exercise. The neighborhood is quiet. Even the birds are less chirpy. Everyone's grass is browning. The steep incline is harder to ascend. My breathing is labored. The pavement feels like burning coals through my shoes. I could fry eggs in a quick minute if I'd only brought a couple with me. I am hot and hemorrhaging water badly. My shirt is drenched. I take it off in hopes of cooling down. The distant rumbling of thunder teases me with the thoughts of the long-promised rain.

sultry air
is heavy with humidity
breathless
—Griffin

haibun art (transforming)
– by Karyn Stockwell

haibun (transforming)

I've never been to the beach in autumn. Indiana Dunes at the south end of Lake Michigan. Deserted. Alone--except for the comfort of your memory. Cloudy. No haze from the steel mills makes Chicago's skyline visible to the west. It's strange wearing jeans and a hoodie instead of shorts and flip flops. Sitting on the soft sand. Digging in, I pull out a pop top ring and the *Snic* section of a Snickers candy bar wrapper. Tuck them into my left pocket to discard later.

I listen to the shore's symphony. Rolling waves splash on the beach, struggling seagulls squawk in the draft, and whistling north winds disturb trees and sand on the dunes. The leaves flip and pop around the sand like a dance troupe. The smell of wet sand and dead fish. Recall coming here as a teenager to tan and meet boys. I remember bringing my kids. A fear of the deep dark water and powerful undertow, I kept them close to shore. My friend's son drowned here. Walking the hard sand at the shoreline, playing tag with the waves. I grab a few colorful stones, some shells, and a small piece of smooth driftwood. Stuff them in my right pocket as souvenirs. Climb halfway up a dune. I feel so minute against the vastness of the water and sky. I smile as your laughter sings in the wind.

wild geese
in chevron flight
passage
— Stockwell

Under the Ginkgo Tree

haibun (transitions)

Kirchhoff city park. Comforting historic trees, cozy wooden benches, and the playground. Stopping to watch the kids jump and dash around. Their laughter is a drug. Background music of birds give harmony to the squeaky swings, squeals from the slide, and shouts of "Faster!" from the merry-go-round. There's a baseball field down the hill. I watch unknown kids play ball. Remembering. I miss days of being a baseball Mom.

It's early autumn. Just a few leaves start the trees' transformation. The bench cradles me as I whiff changes in the air. The sun through the maples creates lace patterns on my arms. A couple, maybe in their seventies, walk along the sidewalk. Holding hands and swinging their arms like young kids. The man's singing, *Unforgettable*, like he's on a Broadway stage. The song ends. They stop. He takes her in his arms, gazes into her eyes, and kisses her like he's a wild and hungry teenager. My eyes tear to share such a moment. The passion and absolute beauty warms my heart. A blazing sunset or star-streaked sky couldn't be more beautiful a sight. A car going by honks at them ... and then another. The man, without lifting his lips from his lady, raises his fist in the air like he'd just won the 100-meter dash in the summer Olympics. His gesture says it all. He has the most coveted prize in his arms. They continue on their walk. His arm around her shoulder, hers around his waist. He starts singing, *It Had To Be You*. Smiling, I hum the song along with him. I leave pleased.

autumn changes
the colors of our days
love stays steadfast
—Stockwell

haibun (serendipity)

Amblin' along the West Fork River. An azure sky above. The daytime moon smiles down at me. Wispy clouds race the wind. Morning sunshine falls like dew between the tall trees. A verdant crown canopy. A lush carpet of verdure beneath my feet. Songbirds fill the warming air with song. Squirrels dig up their buried treasures. Chipmunks play tag among the tall grasses. Geese gossip. Ducks chat. A lone swan glides effortlessly with the river's current. A blue heron walks the river's depths in search of his catch of the day. At the river's edge the fish bubble their greetings, ripples in the water. From a nearby thicket a fawn watches all the comings and goings. People about the path, plugged in, wired up--connected, utter neither a hello nor a good morning in passing. Not even a smile cracks their stony faces. As I walk on, I wonder if they see what I see...

lifting fog
the view clearer
with new eyes
— Barbour

haibun (broken gate)

Wintery sky. Pale. Clouds fan out. Sneaky flurries dash sporadically. A bleak landscape. Flakes cling tenaciously to sturdy grasses. Against mounds of withered corn stalks, wind-blown mini drifts form and reform.

From a nearby copse, a doe, heavily pregnant appears. Motionless, she waits. A sudden noise. Startled. She lifts her head. Ears twitch. A momentary pause. Turns. A single bound, she is out of sight. Back in a safe haven among the trees.

rusty fence
supported by rotted posts
free admittance
—**Brixey**

haibun (the Severn bore)

Our morning constitution. Mist hovers. We clamber over the stile into the orchard. Gather windfalls. Wary fox skulks away. With pockets bulging we continue. Damp leaves cover path. Slippery.   Below us several wooden dinghies left high and dry. Tide's out.

Sound of beating hoofs. Whinnies. Apples proffered. Nuzzles. Laughter. More nuzzles. Pungent smell of wood smoke. Brush piles smolder. Air is still. Along the old tow-path we tarry. Once again, the river is in full-flood. The tidal wave surge has performed.

lightning flash
perched on low branch
kingfisher waits
      — Brixey

Under the Ginkgo Tree

haibun (an early summer garden)

I sit in the shade of the Horse-chestnut tree. The trunk feels warm against my back. Above, white blossoms illuminate the landscape. Soft green leaves offer protection. The sun blazes down from an azure sky. Last night's rain has sweetly perfumed the air. I look around. Everything seems fresh. Born anew. My pencil drops into my lap. I daydream.

dragonflies
hover above the crystal lake
water lilies open

The sweet song of a robin awakens me from my reverie. He has landed close to a clump of Lily of the Valley. An added bonus to the enchantment of this sheltered spot. He pecks at some velvety leaves of a withering primrose plant. A grub or two provide him with a succulent snack.

sweet peas tendrils
adorn the red brick wall
delicate filigree

Groomed borders abut well-manicured lawns. Fresh mulch. Pruned shrubs. No weeds will show their heads here. Lilac bushes sway in the breeze. The sweet scent and purple flowers entice. Several colorful butterflies flit from branch to branch. Carefully selecting the best and fullest stem they land. Lingering just long enough to partake of the nectar offered so freely. Soon I am once again left with my thoughts.

carmine peonies
tower above leafy stems
flamboyant
—**Brixey**

haibun (lost again)

Ok, I've misplaced it again. For the umpteenth time it vanished. Usually, it's my iPhone or my car keys that I lose. Today, it's my pedometer. Frantically, I search. Not on my dresser or in my purse. Upstairs, downstairs...maybe the car? Perhaps my closet? No! Tried all my pockets. Just where did I see it last? If it were my mobile, I'd call it from the house phone. I must get 10,000 steps before midnight.

In desperation, I plop down in the middle of the floor. "Dear God, I know that you know where it is. Please help me". Immediately, I got up and went to my PJ drawer and there it was. Now, how in the world did it get there? I have no idea. But, for future reference, I'll ask Him first.

> what did we do
> before the device age
> we'll never know
> **—Foor**

haibun (reprieve)

Today is my rush, get-everything-done-day. Errands at the college, pharmacy, cleaners, gas station, and market. And Aunt Betty's Cookie Store. Whew, I need to catch my breath. Breathe deeply. Now, a light lunch of roasted turkey breast, baguette, and chilled water. A naval orange for dessert provides the sugar high that I have been needing.

While gazing upon the lawn, I realize I need to get off my duff and finish spreading mulch. Ten cubic yards is one heck of a lot of stuff to move. At one point, I visualized it was looking like the *Mulch of Gibraltar!* Much smaller today. Dark clouds gather to the west. A thunder-clap echoes. BAM! I finish my last wheelbarrow load. Winds gust. Leaves scatter. Precipitation begins to fall in big drops. I run towards the sunroom's door and find escape just before the deluge. With a relaxed sigh, I sit back in my broad wicker chair and close my eyes. What could possibly be better than sipping on a glass of *Afton Cab Sav 14* while listening to the mesmerizing sounds of spring's steady rain?

rain sifts
through trees' emergent leaves
Thoreau nods
— Griffin

haibun (Thelma)

Home. Warm summer evening. We're outside talking away in the carport. Vodka tonics and roasted peanuts nuts by our side. Gerber daisies in full bloom. Her favorite. Red, purple and white petunias flanking the walk. Soft evening light. Impatiens grace the shadows. Flowers' sweet scent abounds. Vibrant colors brighten, soften and warm carport's brick wall and drab concrete. Mama's laughter wafts on evening breeze as we talk of days long gone. I love these times with her. She rocks and talks and sips her tonic — I'm fully engaged. I mix another Grey Goose and ask how long she's been rocking in that old rickety chair. She replies, "All of my life!"

"Now tell me about your new job, and how things are going." With my Mother, it's always a question about me. Unconditional love expressed at every moment, and always set-to-time with every rock of that old oak cane rocker. A perfect four-four.

mama shares
love and life's lessons
life rocks
— Griffin

haibun (flicker)

Campfire cracks and snaps as flames bounce off logs. Burning cedar fills the air with a warm, woodsy scent. Hundreds of glowing embers drift into the cool June night. With tiny bursts of light, they explode and fade. I roast a marshmallow over the coals and taste the warm, gooey sweetness on my tongue. Mesmerized by the fire, the chilly summer night makes me shiver. I wrap an army blanket tighter around my shoulders. Wood smoke and thoughts of you bring tears to my eyes. I yearn to see the fire's light dance on your face.

> lone firefly
> glows in search of mate
> spark dims
> **—Stockwell**

haibun (belonging)

I sneak out of bed to peek between the round posts of the staircase. It's the yearly New Years Eve party at my grandparents' house. Feeling left out, I wonder when I can stay up to celebrate.

Irish reels fill the house with toe-rapping music. Glasses and beer bottles crowd the coffee table. Scents from supper's stew lingers.

From the kitchen, Gramps wears a metal strainer on his head. He leads the parade with a wooden spoon baton. Uncle Bob clashes pot lids. Mom wears her coat backwards and bangs a cake pan. Aunt Marge blows into a coke bottle while Uncle Bill taps a rhythm on the pot she has tied to her backside. The rest of the aunts and uncles have various kitchen utensils and cookware to play in the band. My dad is last. He's wearing a lampshade on his head, Gram's apron, and he's clanging an iron skillet with a meat tenderizer.

Dad spots me. "I know you wanna be with the family." He puts the shade on my head. "C'mon and join the parade, Ayrie."

baby bird watches
as parents teach survival
lessons learned early
—Stockwell

snowman
grins with lusty delight
snowblower's coming

senryu art (snowman)
– art by pixabay.com
– senryu by Stockwell

SENRYU

Senryu, a 13th century Japanese short poetry form, is written in present tense usually over three lines, uses 17 or less syllables, is unrhymed, has no capitalization except for proper nouns, and uses no or minimal punctuation. Sound familiar? Senryu poetry is very similar to the structure of haiku.

Asking Japanese poetry writers to name the difference between haiku and senryu will inevitably bring about a strong debate and many different answers. Like haiku, senryu is written with short/long/short lines using 17 or less syllables. They can include nature, animals, or objects, but the subject must pertain to human elements. Senryu can include a seasonal word (kigo) or a cutting word (kireji), which causes the reader to pause, but aren't required as they are in haiku.

Unlike haiku, senryu writers can use simile, personification, and metaphor. Contrary to many beliefs, senryu does not have to always be humorous. It also uses puns, parody, satire, irony, or silliness (humor) are its usual cornerstones. Many writers use the form to express the misfortunes, adversities and sorrow of people.

So, what is the difference between the two popular forms of Japanese short poetry? Tone. The general character and attitude of senryu relates primarily to the comedy or drama of humans as the underlying essence of the poem.

—**Karyn Stockwell**

205

Under the Ginkgo Tree

the route
of last night's bender
slime trail
—**Barbour**

spoonin'
'till early afternoon
snow day
—**Barbour**

light rain
the old guitarist finger picks
my blues
—**Barbour**

eye of the storm
a pause
in the shouting match
—**Barbour**

daylight savings end
if only I could turn back time
more than one hour
—**Barbour**

morning after
vowing for better or worse
the sound of your snore
— **Barbour**

sifting
through facts and alt-facts
the pooper-scooper
— **Barbour**

campaign promises
the cat
heaves up another hairball
— **Barbour**

this year's resolution
still idle on the treadmill
three weeks later
— **Barbour**

senior class trip
in every window of the bus
a full moon
— **Barbour**

Under the Ginkgo Tree

cinco de mayo
gringo style
margaritas two-for-one
— **Barbour**

thin ice
the depth of modern
relationships
— **Barbour**

hookin' up
a rendezvous
of urges
— **Barbour**

staycation
reacquainting myself
with the backyard
— **Barbour**

nuptial regrets
when "I do"
becomes "Let's fight"
— **Barbour**

bridges to nowhere
the unfulfilled promises
at the campaign's end
— **Barbour**

Saturday night
two-steppin' to the radio
with my cat
— **Barbour**

muffled moans
fill the classroom
today's lesson: writing haiku
— **Barbour**

i-Phone
in the back pocket
smart ass
— **Barbour**

election day
with the flip of a coin
I make my choice
— **Barbour**

Under the Ginkgo Tree

Halloween
the one day each year
I can wear my face
— **Barbour**

cold shower
a temporary fix
for a hot body
— **Barbour**

wastebasket
the file for my poetry
and prose
— **Barbour**

Friday night
I eat fried fish alone
at Burger King
— **Barbour**

morning toilet
the kitten becomes
my coiffeur
— **Barbour**

210

~senryu~

sitting on the curb
drinkin' coffee, shootin' bull
men very hard at work
— **Barbour**

raging waterfall
all the words I wish
I had said
— **Barbour**

going grey
the beautician asks me
who did my highlights
— **Barbour**

hard up, lonely men
seek short-term on-line hookup
wave stiff flags to charm
— **Barbour**

~ • ~

all day rain-
not a single haiku
in the drops

senryu art (all day rain)
— by Diana Barbour

aging woman hopes
to look young in mini skirt
mutton dressed as lamb
— **Brixey**

modern family's
dinner conversation
texting
— **Brixey**

husband tells wife
don't wear long-johns
with sexy nightgowns
— **Brixey**

old man on hot date
leaves Viagra on bureau
feels deflated
— **Brixey**

low slung pants
youth's fashion statement
butt ugly
— **Brixey**

Under the Ginkgo Tree

Oscar night
on the red carpet
Tuxedo Junction
—Foor

matador
wearing montera and cape
dressed to kill
—Foor

edible flowers
grow in graveyard fields
let me eat cake
—Foor

lush greenery
creeps into Kyoto temple
mossy gardens
—Foor

cafe called Karma
has no menu – so you get
what you deserve
—Foor

214

Palominos
gallop across the open meadow
blondes do have more fun
— Foor

blue ship and red ship
collide on the high seas
crews marooned
— Foor

crows kill field mice
it's a case of death
by murder
— Foor

accredited
hospitals and nursing homes
IV league institutions
— Foor

tire went flat
on my drive to work
fork in the road
— Foor

you win a few
occasionally you lose
some princes are frogs
—Foor

mermaid met musician
under the boardwalk
both loved scales
—Foor

Amsterdam
ladies of the night
window dressing
—Foor

angler
is allergic to fish
herring impaired
—Foor

Grandma bought
goose feather pillows
no down payment
—Foor

216

flunked exam
at magician school
trick questions
— Foor

learned to make
delicious ice cream
Sunday school
— Foor

shoemakers
wed in spring
sole-mates
— Foor

King Arthur
famous for his round table
and his knight life
— Foor

tennis player
never married
love meant nothing
— Foor

Under the Ginkgo Tree

headhunters
bury their victims
skullduggery
— **Foor**

annulment
granted to banker and wife
lack of interest
— **Foor**

though father time
may be a great healer
he's a lousy beautician
— **Foor**

successful mortician
buys crystal glass coffins
remains to be seen
— **Foor**

~ • ~

nude swimmers
frolic in starlit waters
moonlighting
    —**Griffin**

Waiting in queue
for fried dough at fair's food booth
waisted line
    —**Griffin**

blue hairs socialize
at Plaza's afternoon high tea
slim pickings
    —**Griffin**

watch for poisonous
snakes if you need to pee
prairie rest stops
    —**Griffin**

three thousand
miles by car in five days
flat-ass-itis
    —**Griffin**

Under the Ginkgo Tree

a politician
by and for the people
right after himself
—Johnson

clumsy elephants
stomp, snort, accomplish nothing
donkeys are asses
—Johnson

congressional clowns
perform circus sideshow
to avoid governance
—Johnson

dating website
worst place to search for
a good-night kiss
—Johnson

my life
a jigsaw puzzle with a few
pieces missing
—Johnson

Keep Right on Writing -On

Debbie Johnson

Though I loved reading and writing during my school years, adult life was filled with other activities. I was disabled in 2004 and afterward, had the opportunity to take a therapeutic writing class for the disabled. I later joined a therapeutic writing group which I now facilitate.

My initial goal with writing was to share the experience of disability in prose. After reading poetry, my love for it grew and much of my writing is now poetry. A newcomer to poetry, I yearned to learn about it and the myriad of forms that exist. Looking simple to a newcomer, I learned the complexities of writing JSF with some very skilled teachers.

For me, writing is a therapeutic activity, a passion, a creative process, and advocation, and yes, probably an addiction. It has also connected me with writers and editors around the globe. I am uncomfortable whenever I am without a notebook and pen, never knowing what might inspire a poem or story. Happy and sad, good and bad can all provide the spark for me to write. Writing is a daily activity and a very important aspect of my life.

My motto is 'Keep Right on Writing On'.

—DJ

cemetery
beside busy train tracks
souls won't rest in peace
—**Johnson**

piercing eyes
look of disgust reveals
no insight
—**Johnson**

husband and wife
argue without reason
cross-words puzzling
—**Johnson**

reality TV
what we turn to when we
have abandoned life
—**Johnson**

some find pearls
my luck gives only empty
clam shells
—**Johnson**

beagles can sense
changes in a woman's mood
men don't have a clue
—**Johnson**

men-o-pause
the age at which men
begin to slow down
—**Johnson**

a hopeless romantic
she is always in love
with her mirror
—**Johnson**

a poor man
works hard at the pizza parlor
rolling in the dough
—**Johnson**

I no longer
insert foot in mouth, now settle
for just a shoe
—**Johnson**

Under the Ginkgo Tree

I wait for my ship
to come in-- one thousand miles
from nearest ocean
—**Johnson**

my smartphone
must go—it's become
a wise-ass
—**Johnson**

police awaken
sailor sleeping on the beach
tequila sunrise
—**Johnson**

U.S. Capitol dome
has thirteen hundred cracks
just like senator's heads
—**Johnson**

braless revolution
exposes to all
bosom buddies
—**Johnson**

224

after two a.m.
sleeping pill commercials
put you to sleep
—**Johnson**

clutching her chest
with a deep sigh she felt
a heart-attract
—**Johnson**

after cleaning
the once cobweb-filled attic
cranial atrophy
—**Johnson**

happy bluebird
chirps innocently from tree
white goop in my hair
—**Johnson**

bridge over troubled water
politician under suspicion
prepares to jump
—**Johnson**

Under the Ginkgo Tree

the best part
of in-law's visiting
tail lights
— **Stockwell**

mountain winter storm
brings welcome isolation
wish you were here
— **Stockwell**

single red rose
delivered with love note
I check address — twice
— **Stockwell**

expensive clothes bought
for girlfriend's fun night out
no money for drinks
— **Stockwell**

sexy lingerie
bought to spice up romance
price tags still on
— **Stockwell**

kids watermelon
seed-spitting contest at picnic
mom joins in
— **Stockwell**

they greet the day
with sizzling passion
oh what a beautiful moaning
— **Stockwell**

best friend's number
still on phone after death
just can't delete
— **Stockwell**

young boy shouts
into whirling fan
sound effects
— **Stockwell**

bride walks with wonder
to her soon-to-be husband
organ plays death march
— **Stockwell**

227

with hope
we gave him keys to the nation
time to change the locks
— Stockwell

cloud animals
parade across summer sky
child's mind creates a zoo
— Stockwell

dear Santa baby
I've enough playtime toys
please bring batteries
— Stockwell

death accepted as
a good reason to miss work
notice required
— Stockwell

couples cuddle
during February's freeze
November baby boom
— Stockwell

it's easy to spot
lovey-dovey newlyweds
mush ad-nauseam
— Stockwell

moment of wisdom
learning life's not always sweet
sour discovery
— Stockwell

foreplay begins
night of passionate hunger
appetizers
— Stockwell

Viagra's magic
endows powerful new life
never lets you down
— Stockwell

when your heart
is slashed into hundreds of pieces
scraps make a great quilt
— Stockwell

229

you warm my bed
more than a hot water bottle
toasty spooning
—Stockwell

mother and daughter
spend snow day cooking, laughing
love thick as pea soup
—Stockwell

rainbow Jell-O
brought to funeral luncheon
colors in sea of black
—Stockwell

pain and bruises
from trips over your hurdles
at last...over you
—Stockwell

politicians banned
from kissing any babies
grimy mud-slingers
—Stockwell

tiptoeing
over life's slippery rocks
belly flop ballet
— **Stockwell**

with invisible
eyes in the back of her head
mom always caught me
— **Stockwell**

woman makes
milestone birthday wish
candles stay lit
— **Stockwell**

Purple Heart
graces her dress uniform
posthumous
— **Stockwell**

~ • ~

they turn from truth
in search of obtuse voters
mendacity

ethical well
sucked dry by avarice
poly-ticks

senryu suite art (mendacity)
– art by pixabay.com
– senryu by Ray Griffin

SENRYU SUITE

The senryu suite follows the same guidelines as provided in the previous section for senryu. Senryu can be written as a suite of poems. The suite of senryu must relate to each other and provide larger story than a single senryu could convey. Each senryu must also be able to stand on its own.

—**Karyn Stockwell**

senryu suite (spicy chili)

politicians
pledge energy independence
equivocators

forty years
of federal fecklessness
electile dysfunction

spicy chili
and energy policy
natural gas
—**Griffin**

Under the Ginkgo Tree

senryu suite (tyranny)

politicians use
weasel words to deceive us
1984

when one seeks office
for sake of self, and power
democracy wanes

he betrays
our values of liberty
Jefferson weeps

autocrats deconstruct
democracy's institutions
DEFCON 1

when we do not act
before it becomes too late
Kristallnacht
— Griffin

senryu suite (in Katrina's wake)

in Katrina's wake
people shout, shove, steal and kill
animal instinct

amidst earthquake's
debris Japanese are calm; caring
civilized culture

the world is a stage
national norms on display
the envelope, please
— Griffin

Under the Ginkgo Tree

senryu suite (zombie a-pock-a-lips)

zombie serenades
victim with banjo
brain picker

naughty zombie
exposes flesh to prey
brain tease

ninja zombie
stealthily sneaks up on geek
brainiac attack

zombie plunges
into clogged skull
brain drain

beauty queen
shuffles in zombie parade
brain waves

zombie hunts
for food during blizzard
brain storm

zombie collapses
during marathon scuffle
brain cramp

drenched zombie
plods through snowstorm
brain freeze

grimy zombie
dives into blood bath
brain washed

toddler zombie
devours sour patch kids
brain child
—**Stockwell**

petals
flutter in gentle breeze
circadian beauty

haiga (petals)
— by Ann Brixey

INDEX

Made in the USA
Las Vegas, NV
21 December 2022

63780767R00144